Jimmy Sniffles
Up the President's Nose

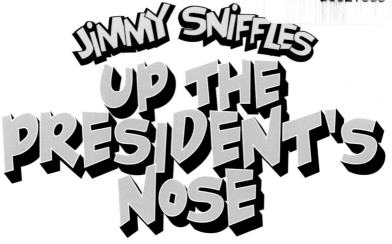

Librarian Reviewer
Katharine Kan
Graphic novel reviewer and Library Consultant, Panama City, FL
MLS in Library and Information Studies, University of Hawaii at Manoa, HI

Reading Consultant
Elizabeth Stedem
Educator/Consultant, Colorado Springs, CO
MA in Elementary Education, University of Denver, CO

STONE ARCH BOOKS
MINNEAPOLIS SAN DIEGO

Graphic Sparks are published by Stone Arch Books
151 Good Counsel Drive, P.O. Box 669
Mankato, Minnesota 56002
www.stonearchbooks.com

Library of Congress Cataloging-in-Publication Data
Nickel, Scott.
Up the President's Nose / by Scott Nickel; illustrated by Steve Harpster.
p. cm. — (Graphic Sparks. Jimmy Sniffles)
ISBN-13: 978-1-59889-837-8 (library binding)
ISBN-10: 1-59889-837-X (library binding)
ISBN-13: 978-1-59889-893-4 (paperback)
ISBN-10: 1-59889-893-0 (paperback)
1. Graphic novels. I. Harpster, Steve. II. Title.
PN6727.N544U6 2008
741.5'973—dc22 2007003179

Summary: The president is suffering a strange allergic reaction. His life could be in danger! Jimmy Sniffles, the kid who knows noses, is shrunk down to microscopic size to sniff out the problem. Look out! Evil lurks within the presidential nostrils.

Art Director: Heather Kindseth
Graphic Designer: Brann Garvey

1 2 3 4 5 6 12 11 10 09 08 07

Printed in the United States of America

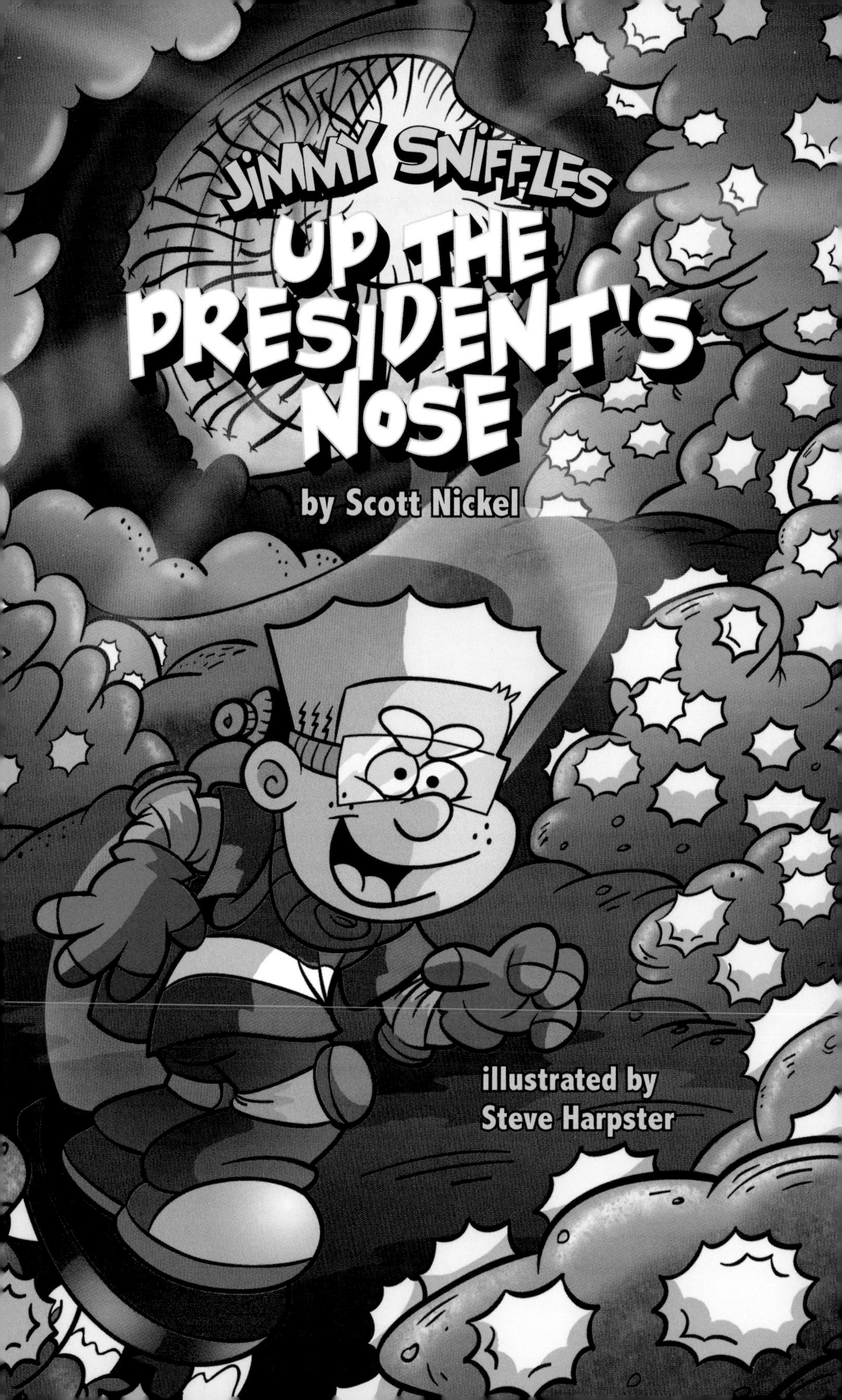

JIMMY SNIFFLES
UP THE PRESIDENT'S NOSE
by Scott Nickel
illustrated by
Steve Harpster

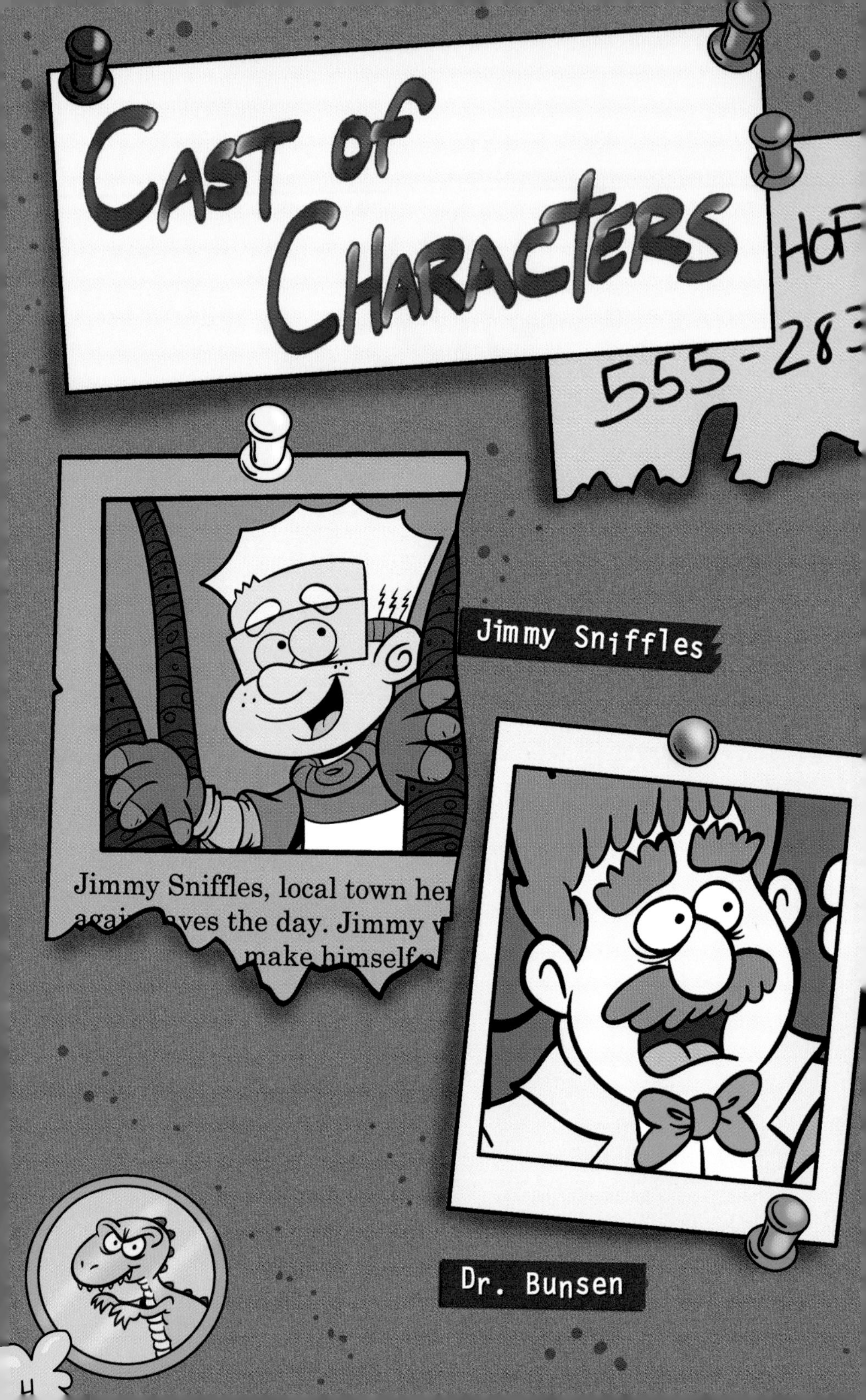

Cast of Characters
HOF
555-283
Jimmy Sniffles
Jimmy Sniffles, local town her
aves the day. Jimmy w
make himself
Dr. Bunsen

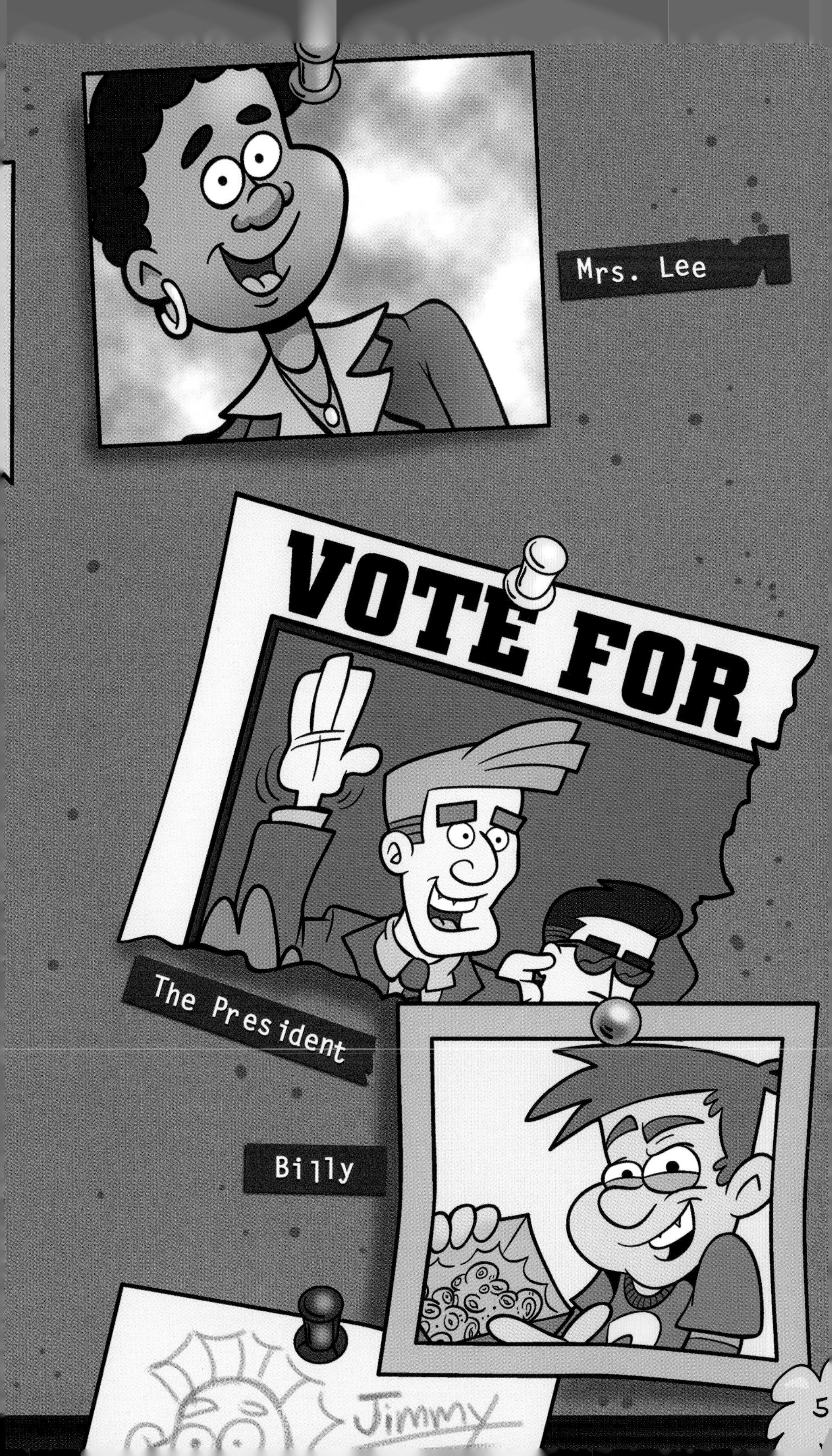
Mrs. Lee
VOTE FOR
The President
Billy
Jimmy

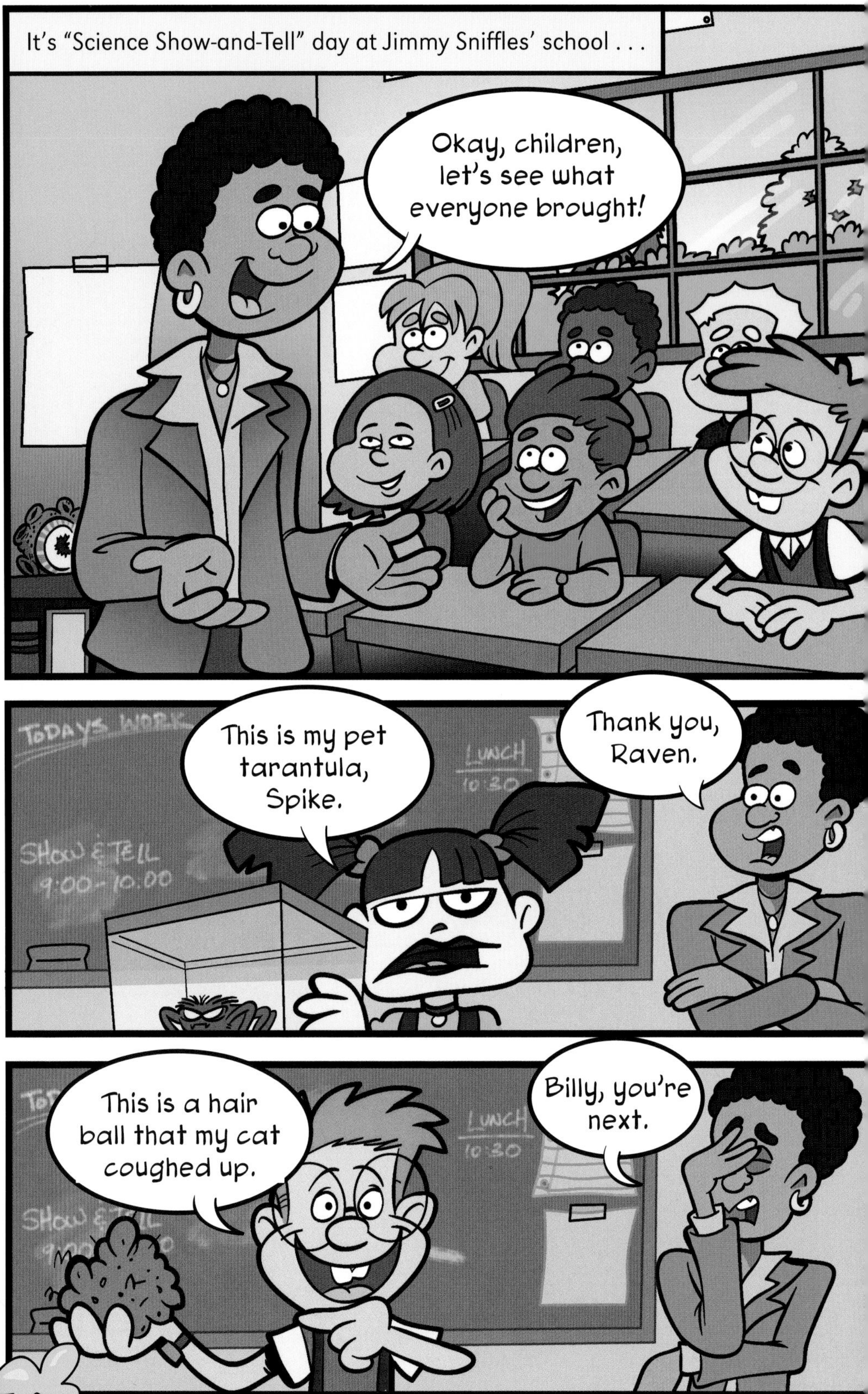
It's "Science Show-and-Tell" day at Jimmy Sniffles' school . . .
Okay, children, let's see what everyone brought!
TODAYS WORK
LUNCH 10:30
SHOW & TELL 9:00–10.00
This is my pet tarantula, Spike.
Thank you, Raven.
This is a hair ball that my cat coughed up.
Billy, you're next.

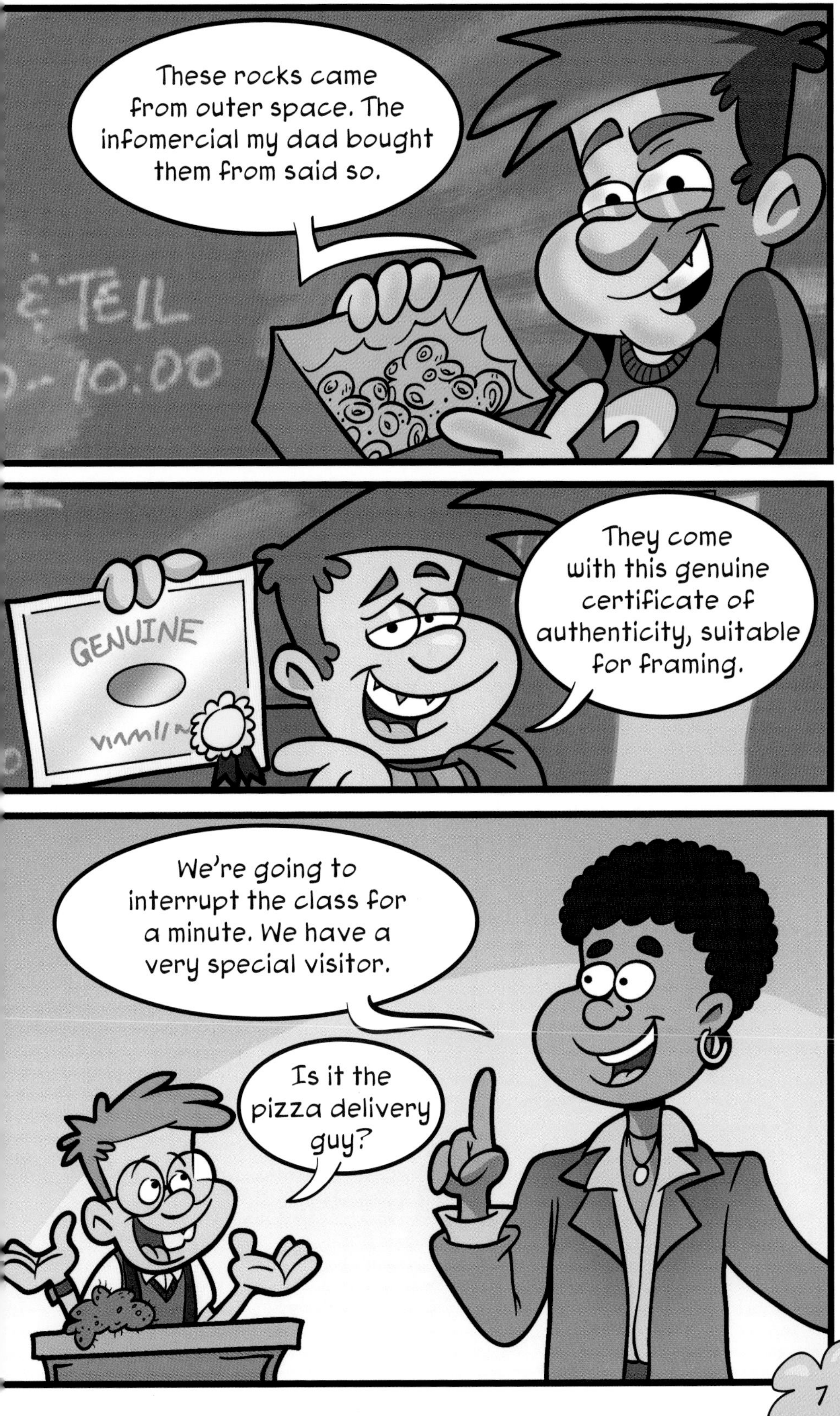
& TELL
-10:00
These rocks came from outer space. The infomercial my dad bought them from said so.
GENUINE
They come with this genuine certificate of authenticity, suitable for framing.
We're going to interrupt the class for a minute. We have a very special visitor.
Is it the pizza delivery guy?

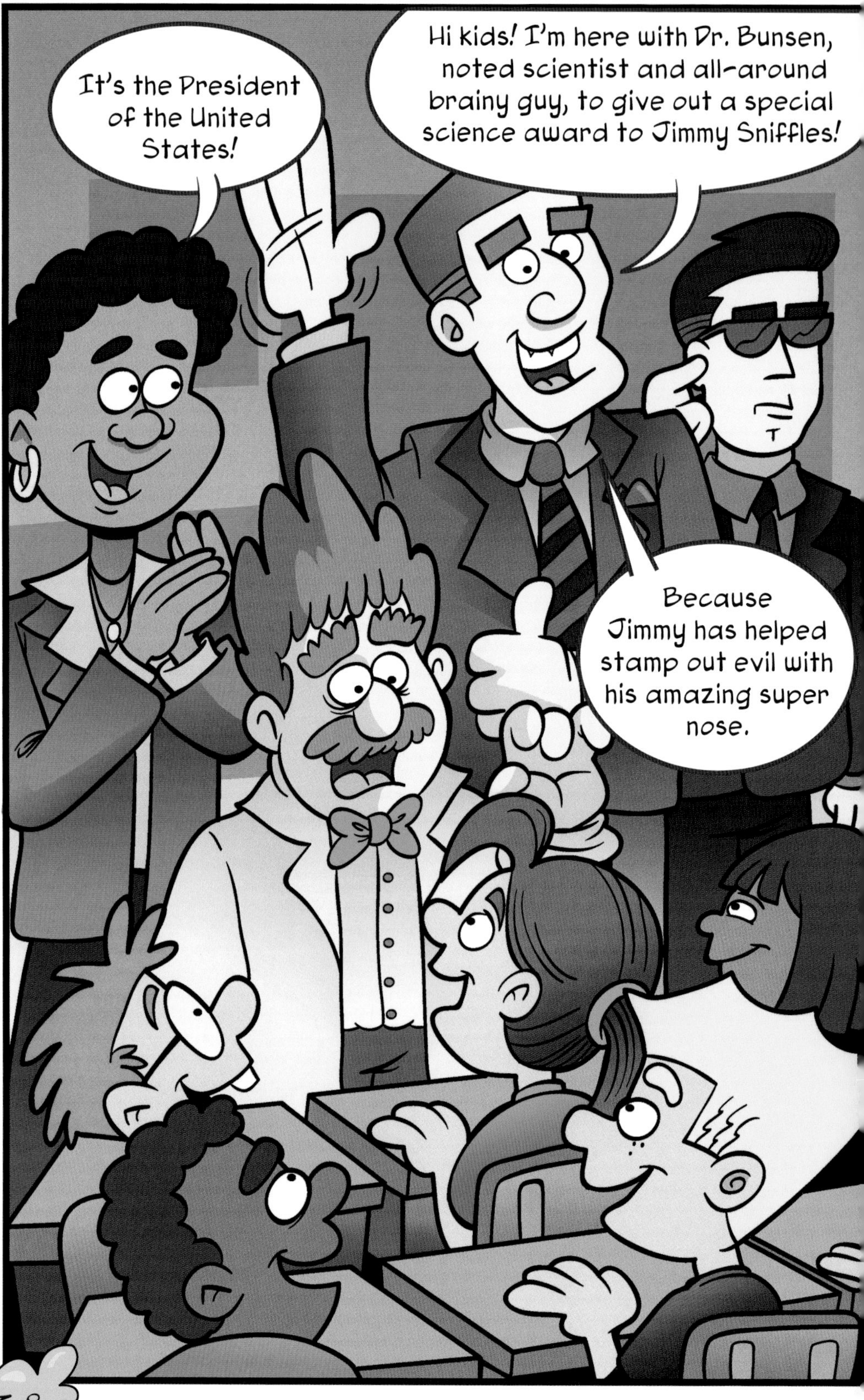
It's the President of the United States!
Hi kids! I'm here with Dr. Bunsen, noted scientist and all-around brainy guy, to give out a special science award to Jimmy Sniffles!
Because Jimmy has helped stamp out evil with his amazing super nose.

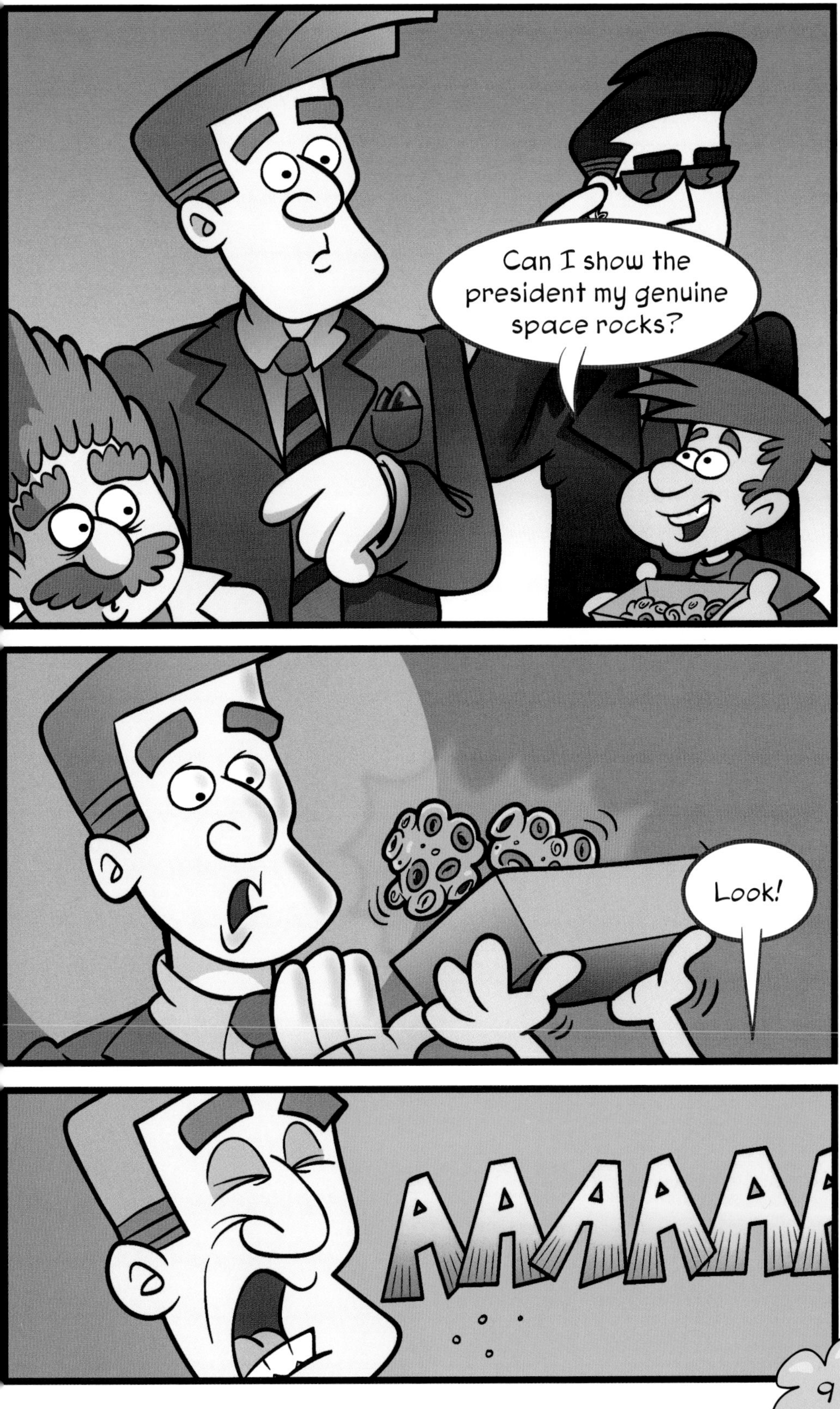
Can I show the president my genuine space rocks?
Look!
AAAAA

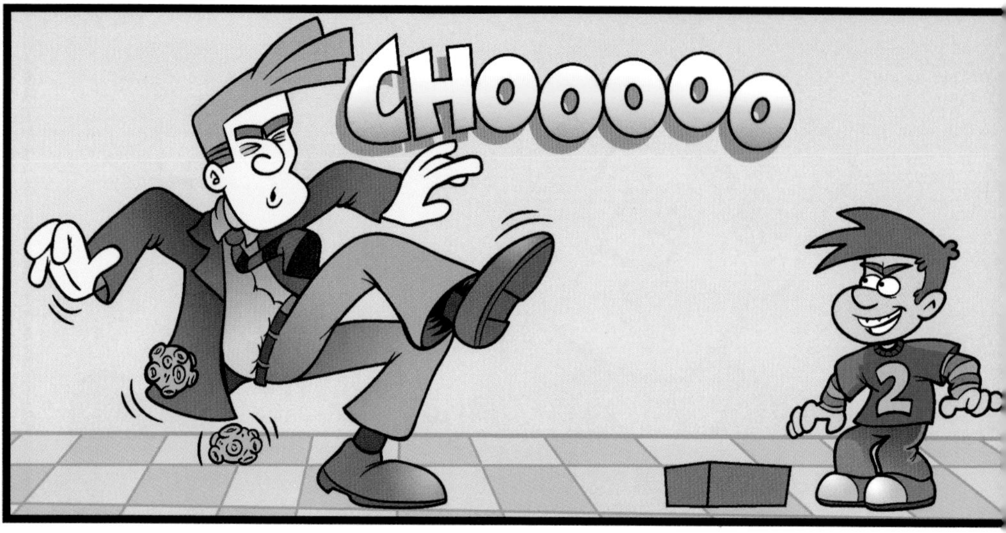
CHOOOOO

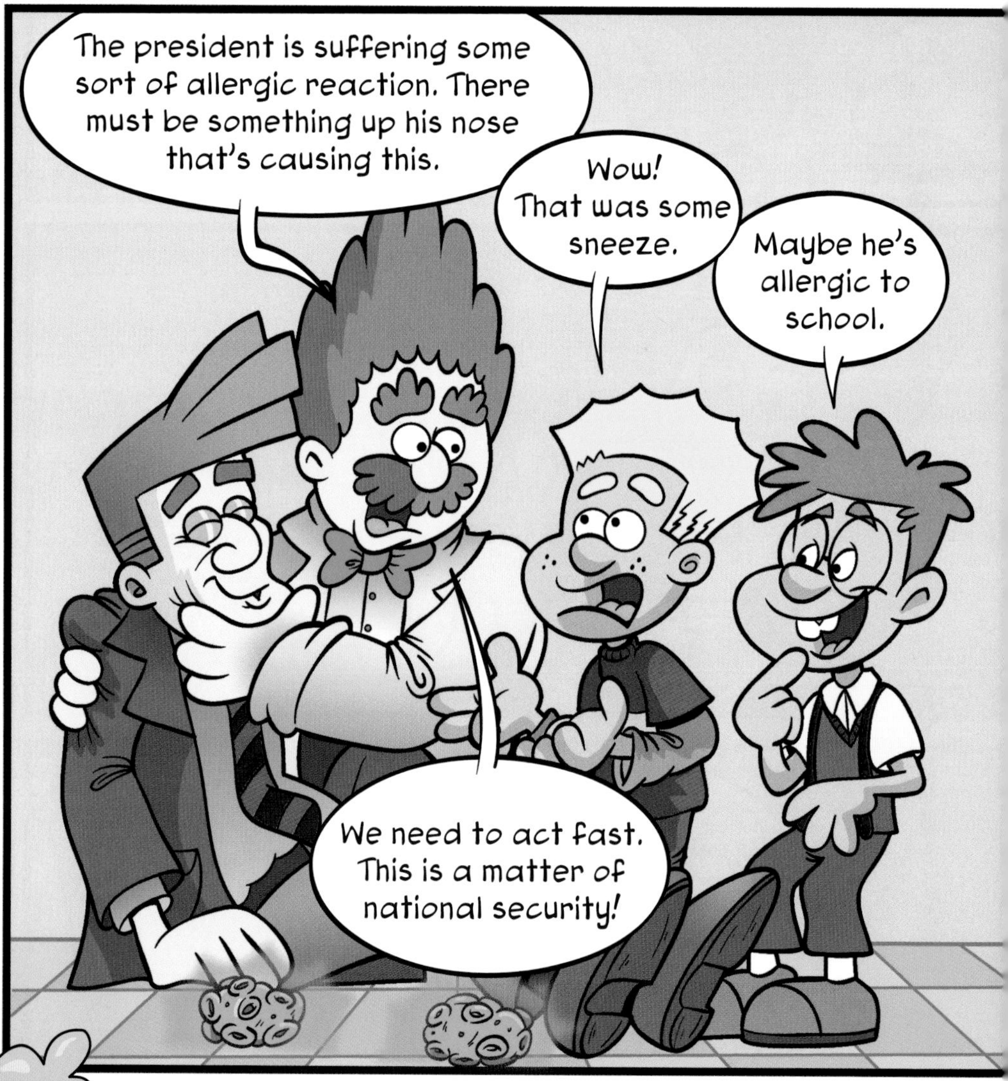
The president is suffering some sort of allergic reaction. There must be something up his nose that's causing this.
Wow! That was some sneeze.
Maybe he's allergic to school.
We need to act fast. This is a matter of national security!

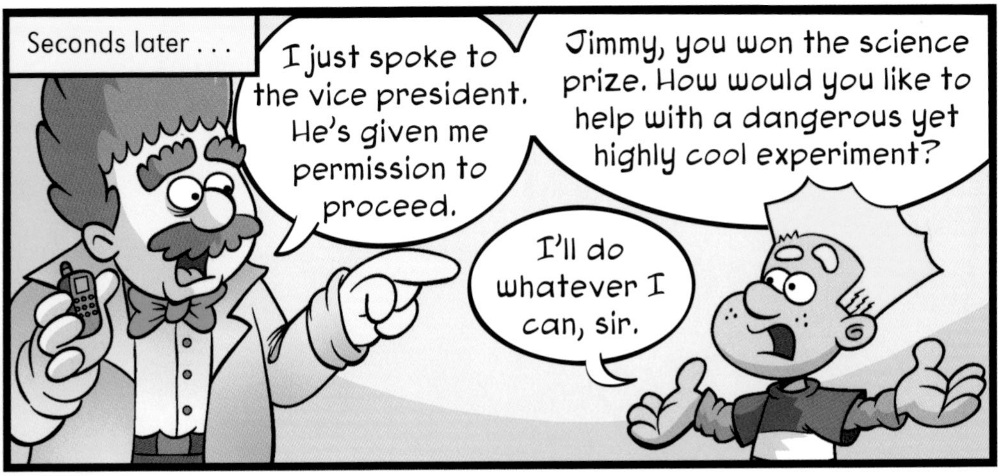
Seconds later . . .
I just spoke to the vice president. He's given me permission to proceed.
Jimmy, you won the science prize. How would you like to help with a dangerous yet highly cool experiment?
I'll do whatever I can, sir.

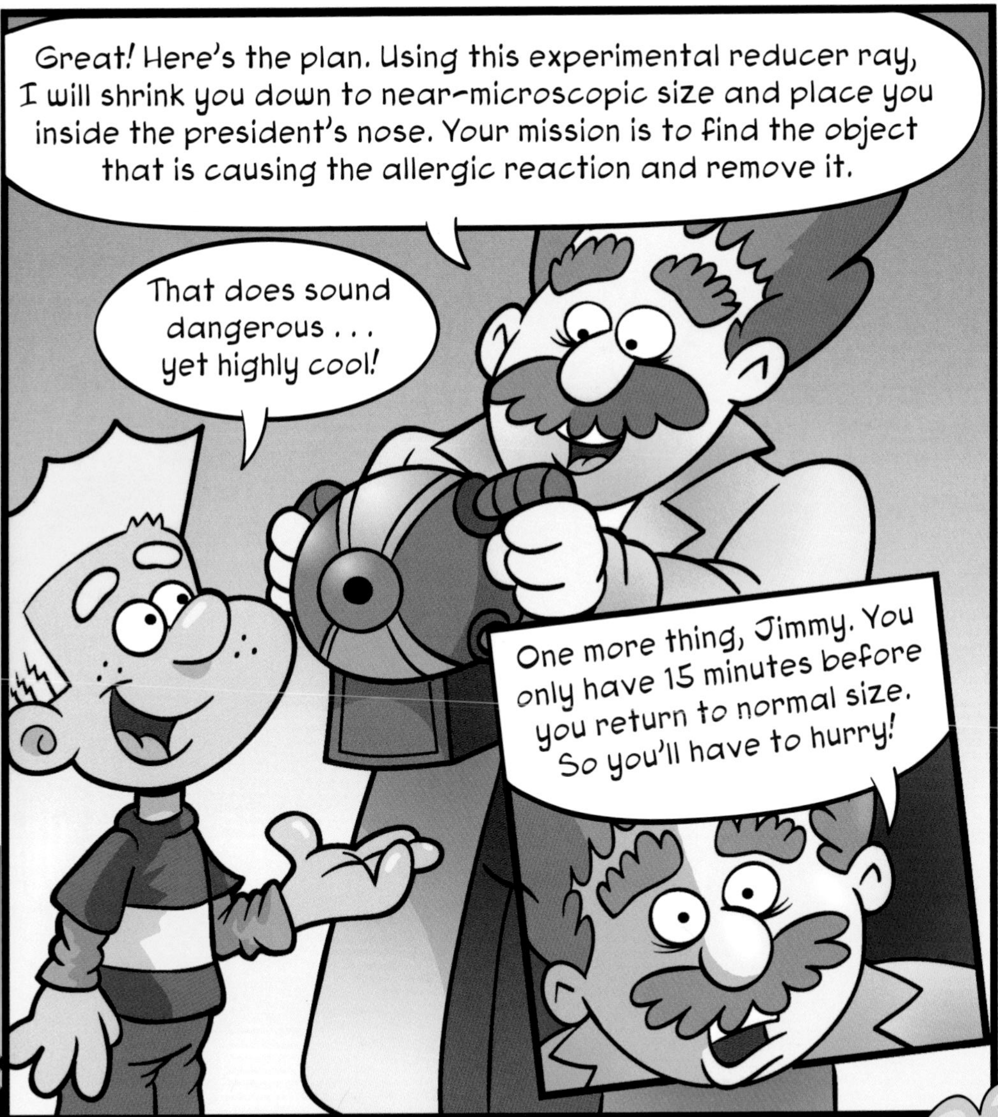
Great! Here's the plan. Using this experimental reducer ray, I will shrink you down to near-microscopic size and place you inside the president's nose. Your mission is to find the object that is causing the allergic reaction and remove it.
That does sound dangerous . . . yet highly cool!
One more thing, Jimmy. You only have 15 minutes before you return to normal size. So you'll have to hurry!

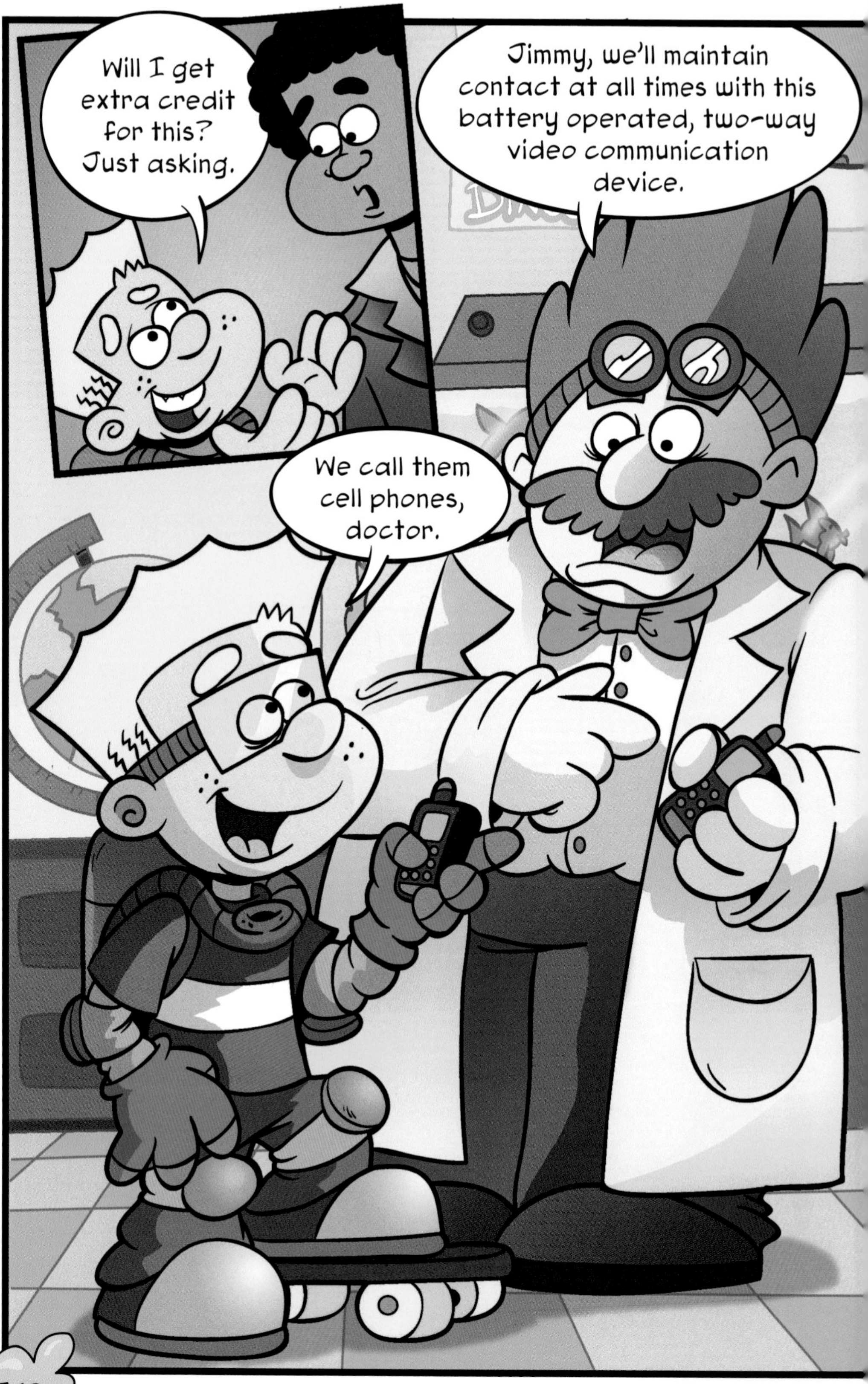
Will I get extra credit for this? Just asking.
Jimmy, we'll maintain contact at all times with this battery operated, two-way video communication device.
We call them cell phones, doctor.

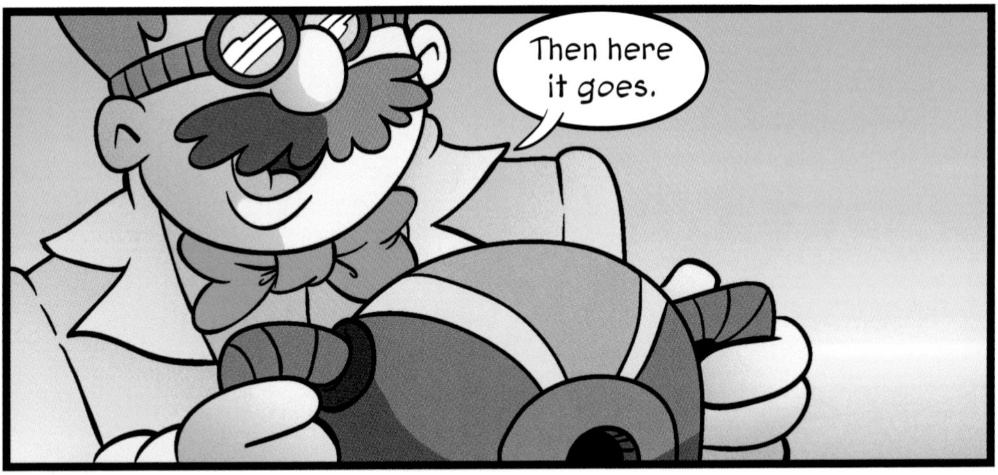
Then here it goes.

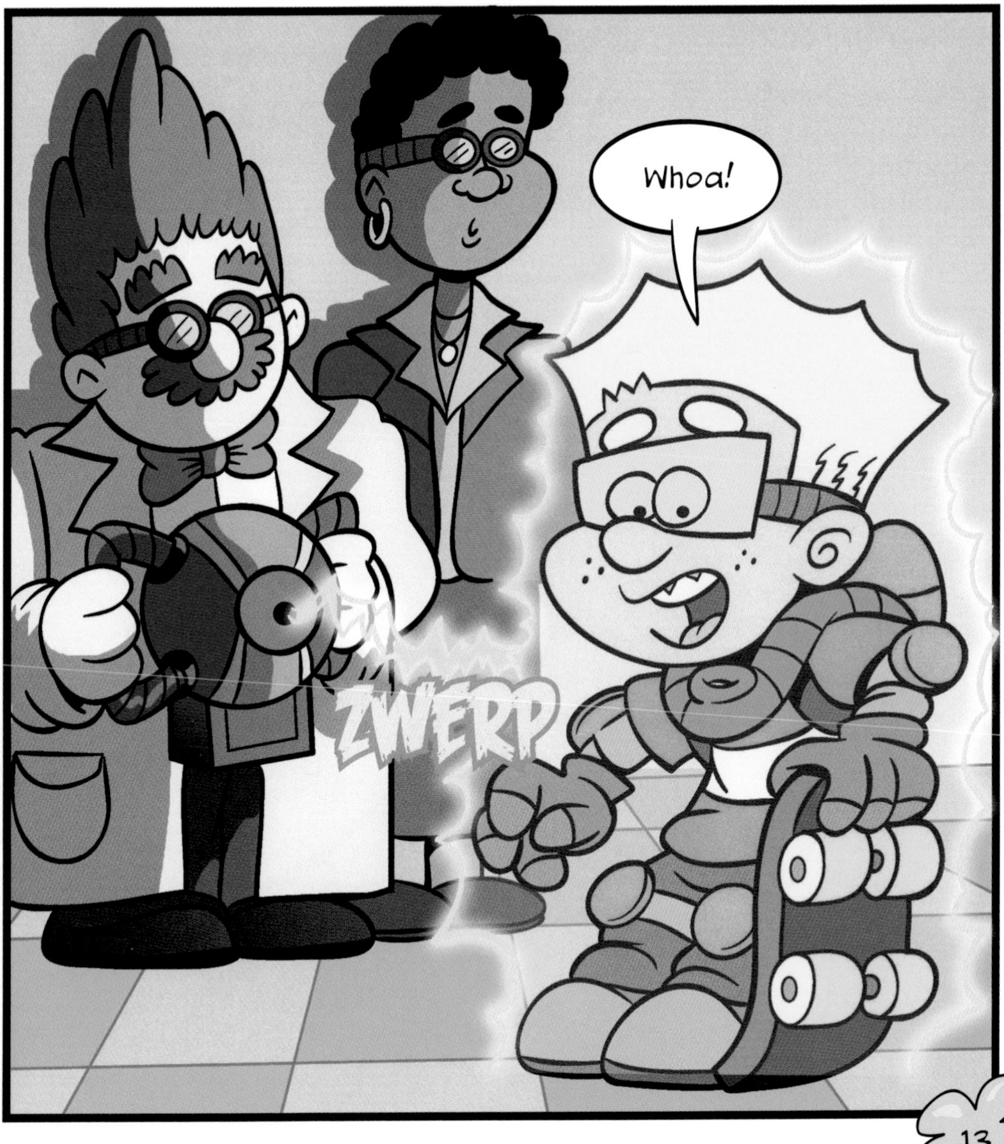
Whoa!
ZWERP

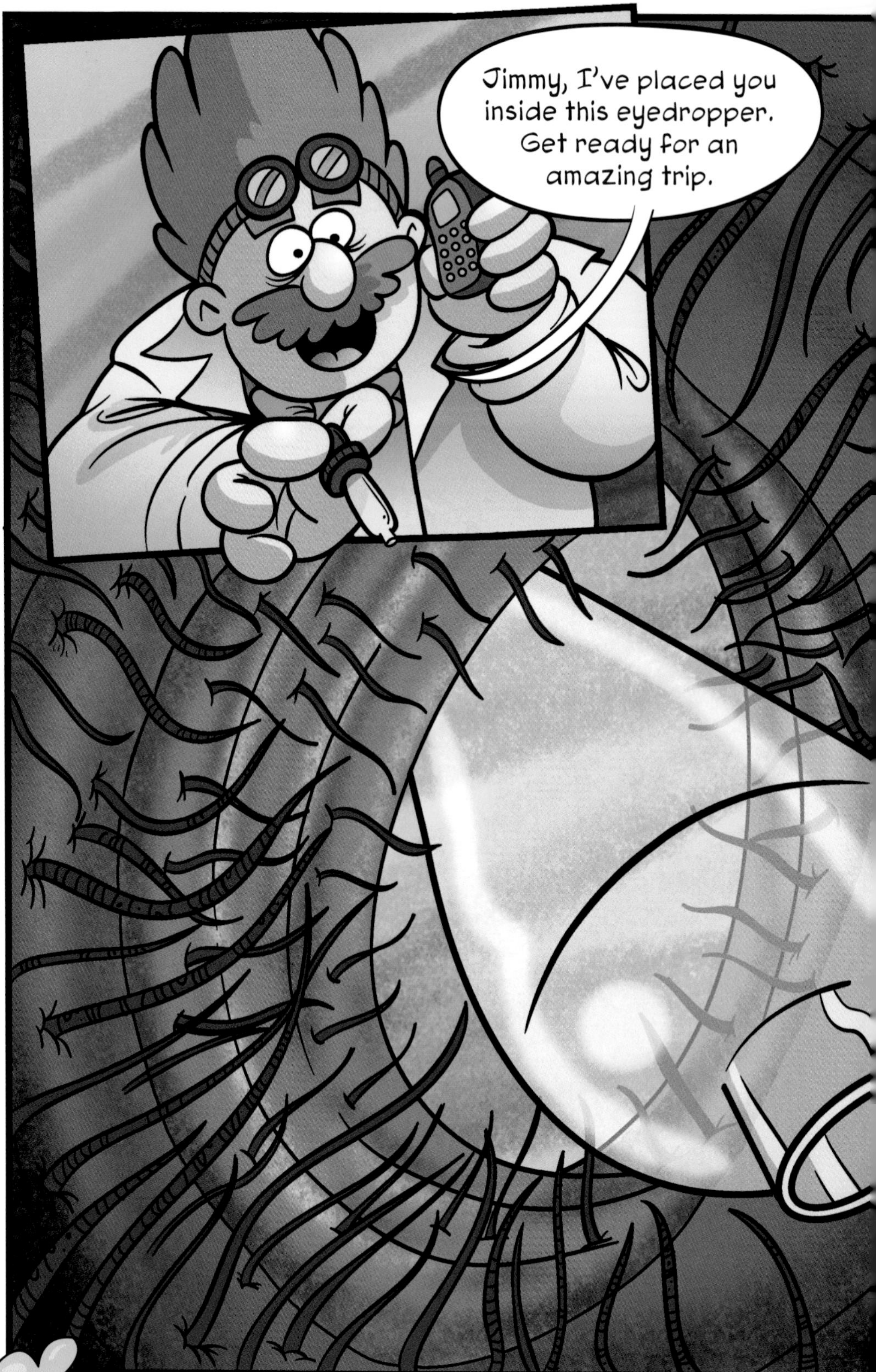
Jimmy, I've placed you inside this eyedropper. Get ready for an amazing trip.

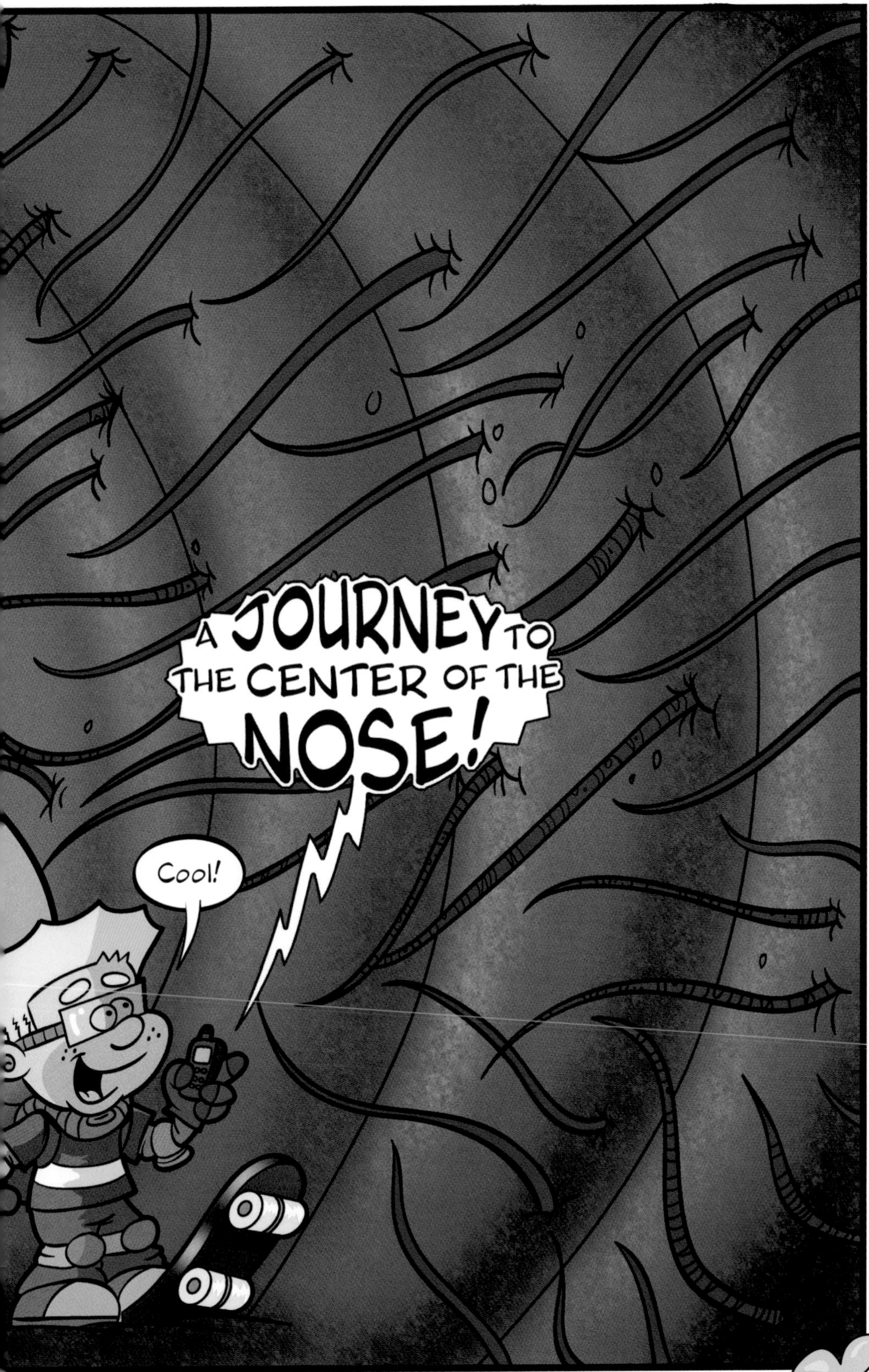
A JOURNEY TO THE CENTER OF THE NOSE!
Cool!

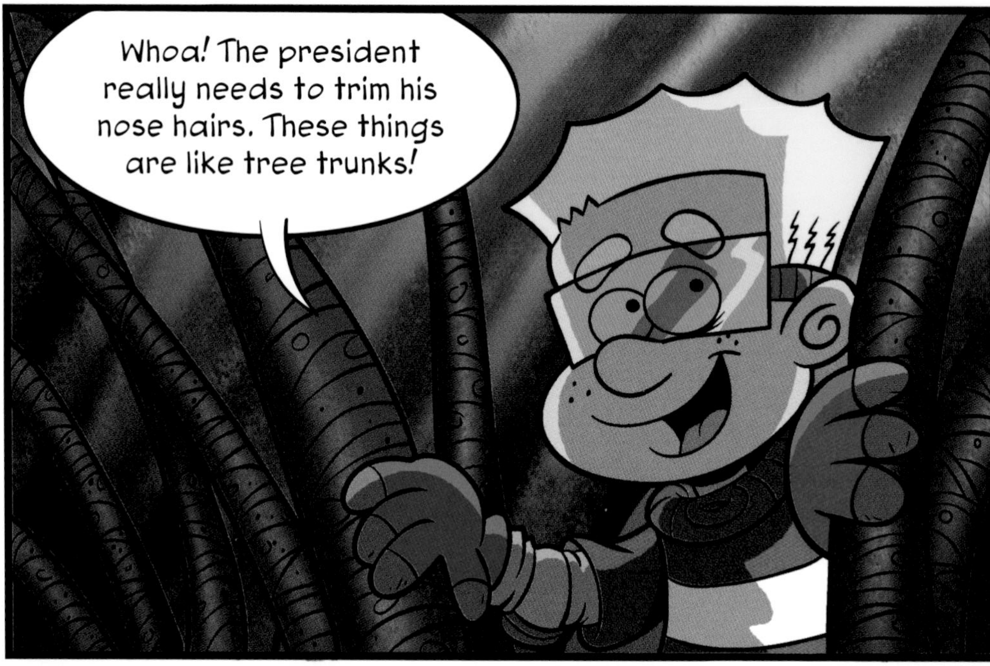
Whoa! The president really needs to trim his nose hairs. These things are like tree trunks!

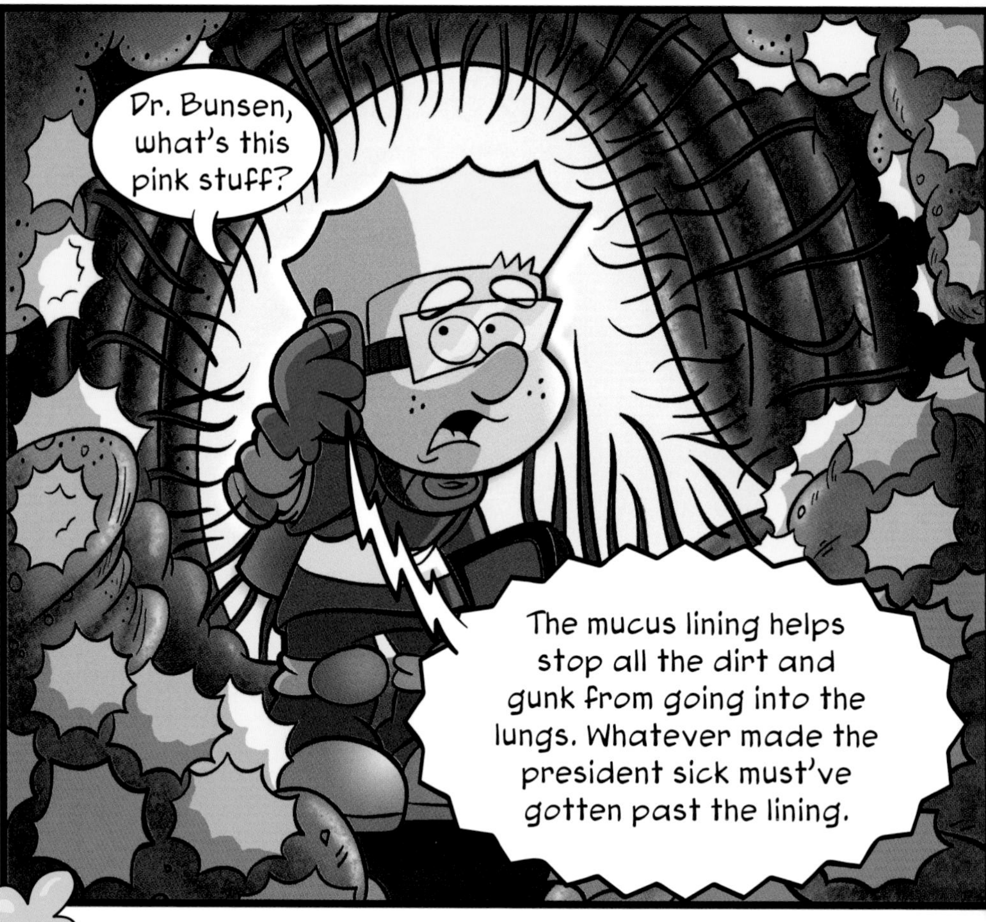
Dr. Bunsen, what's this pink stuff?
The mucus lining helps stop all the dirt and gunk from going into the lungs. Whatever made the president sick must've gotten past the lining.

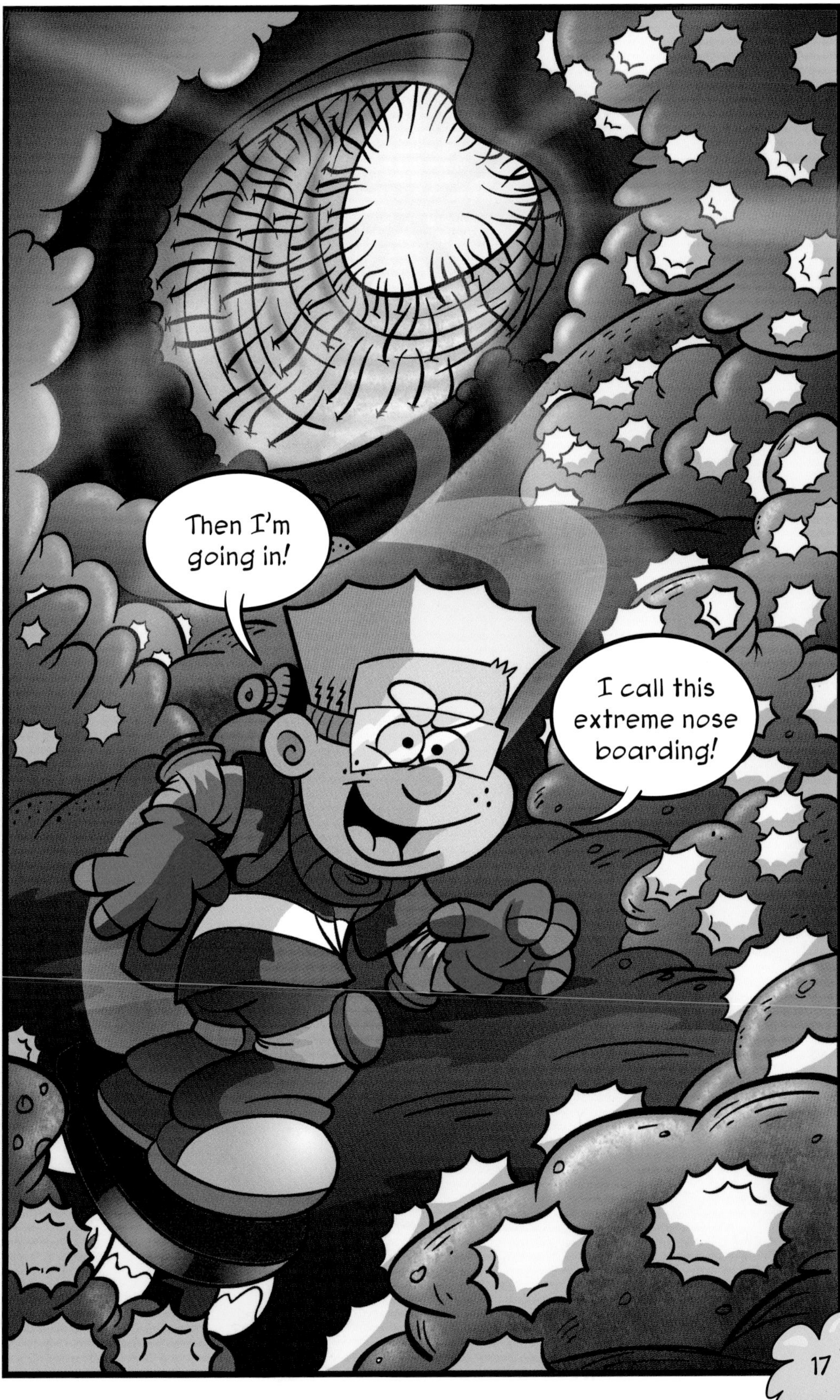
Then I'm going in!
I call this extreme nose boarding!

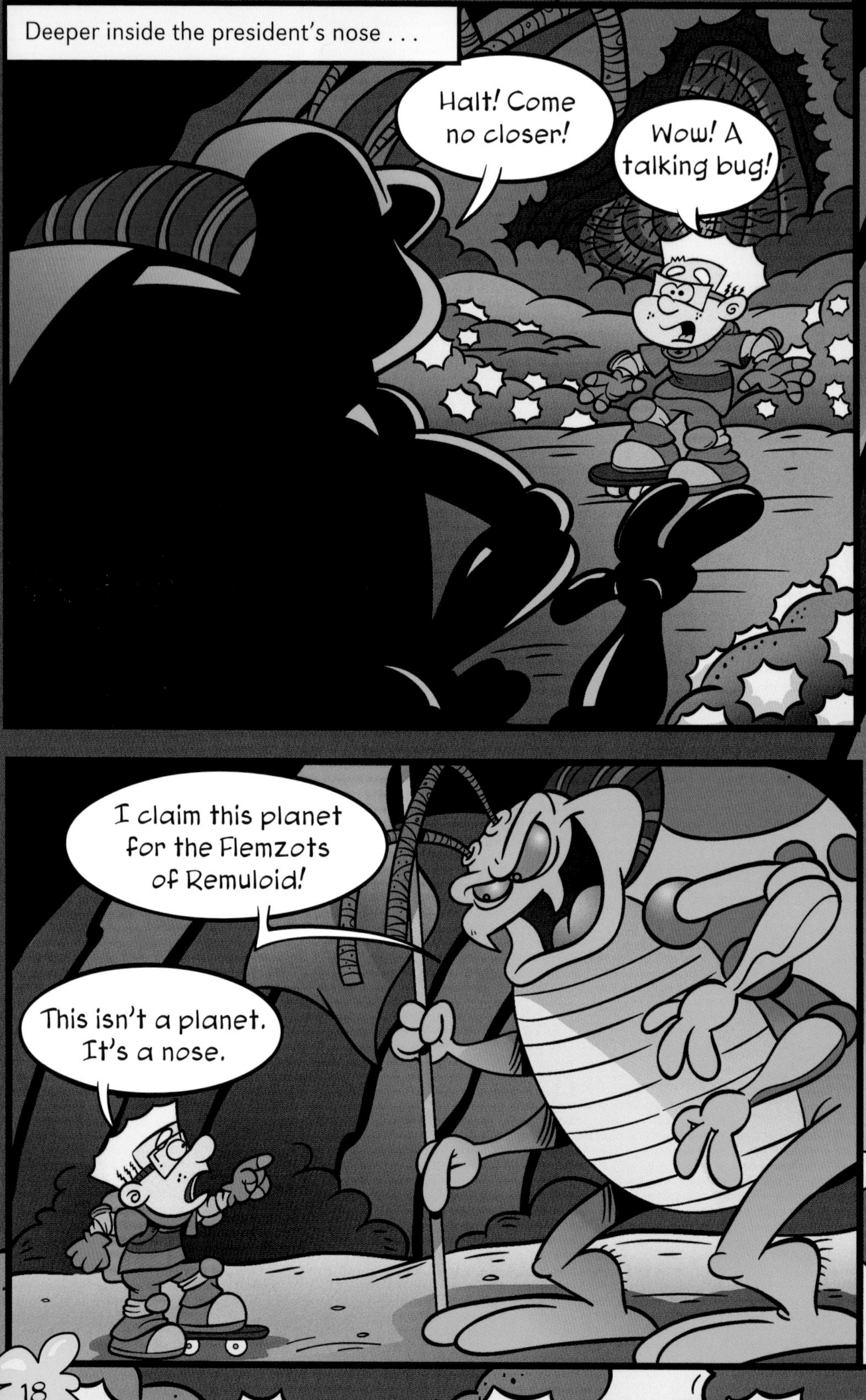
Deeper inside the president's nose . . .
Halt! Come no closer!
Wow! A talking bug!
I claim this planet for the Flemzots of Remuloid!
This isn't a planet. It's a nose.

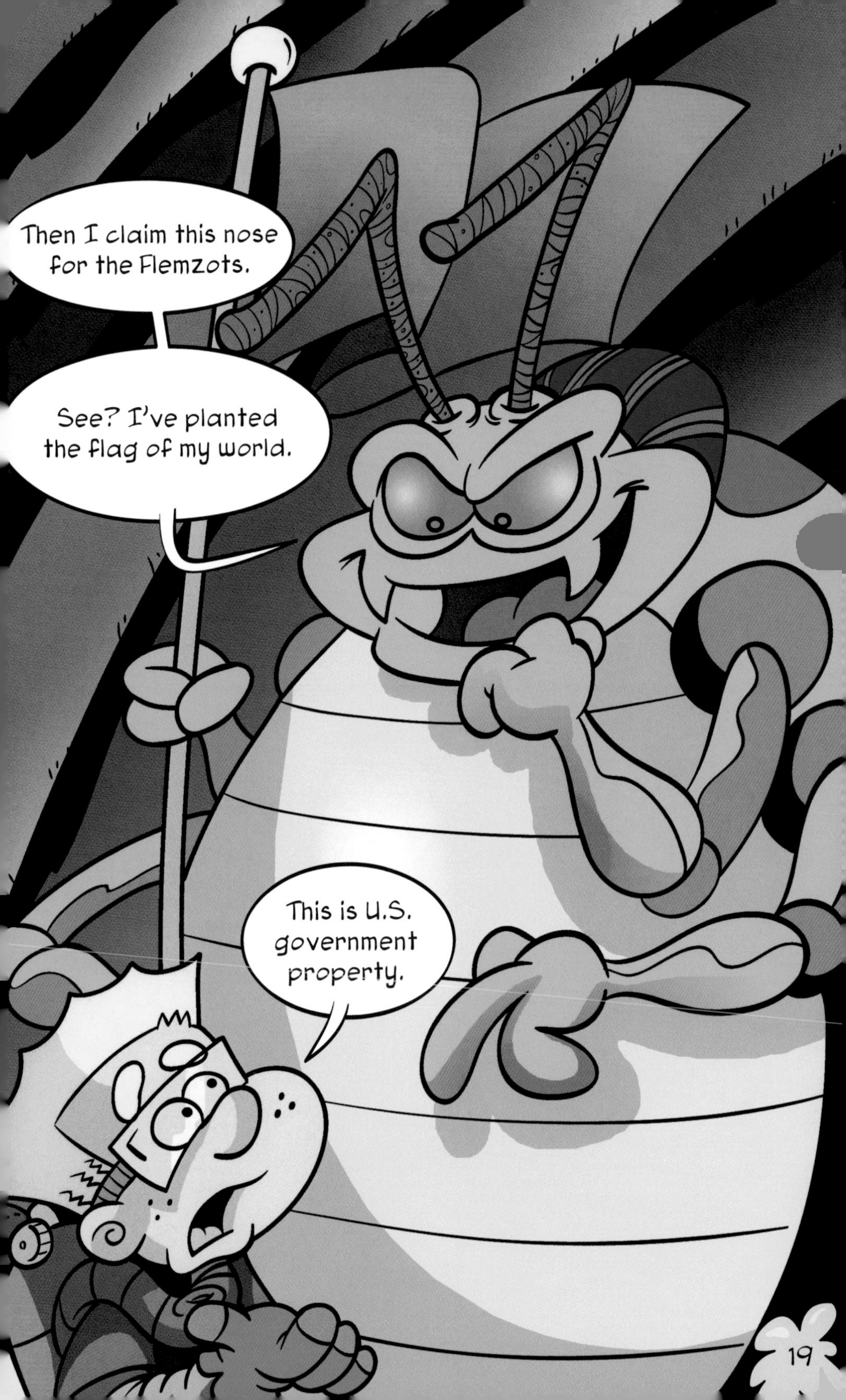
Then I claim this nose for the Flemzots.
See? I've planted the flag of my world.
This is U.S. government property.

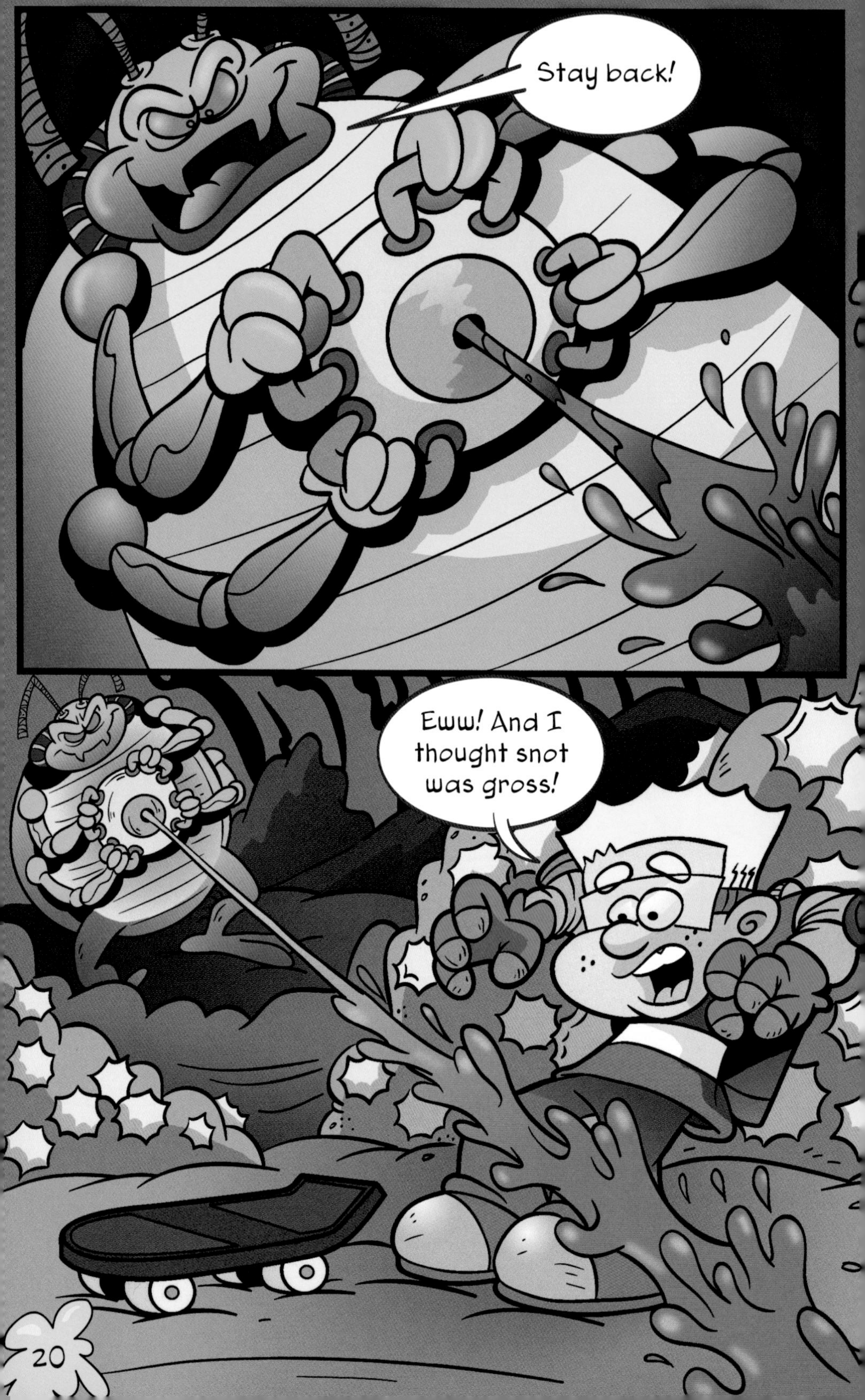

Stay back!
Eww! And I thought snot was gross!

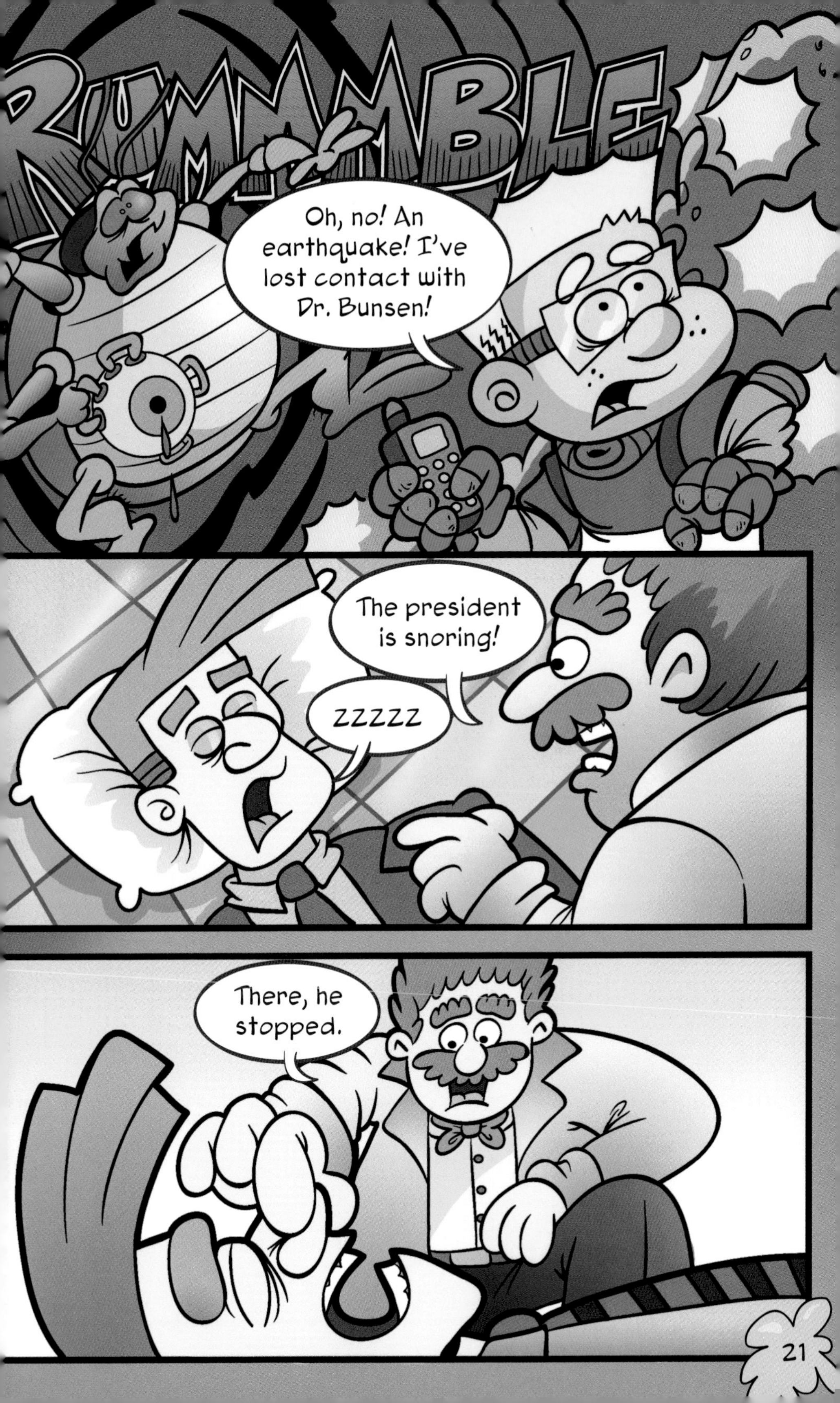
RUMMMBLE
Oh, no! An earthquake! I've lost contact with Dr. Bunsen!
The president is snoring!
ZZZZZ
There, he stopped.

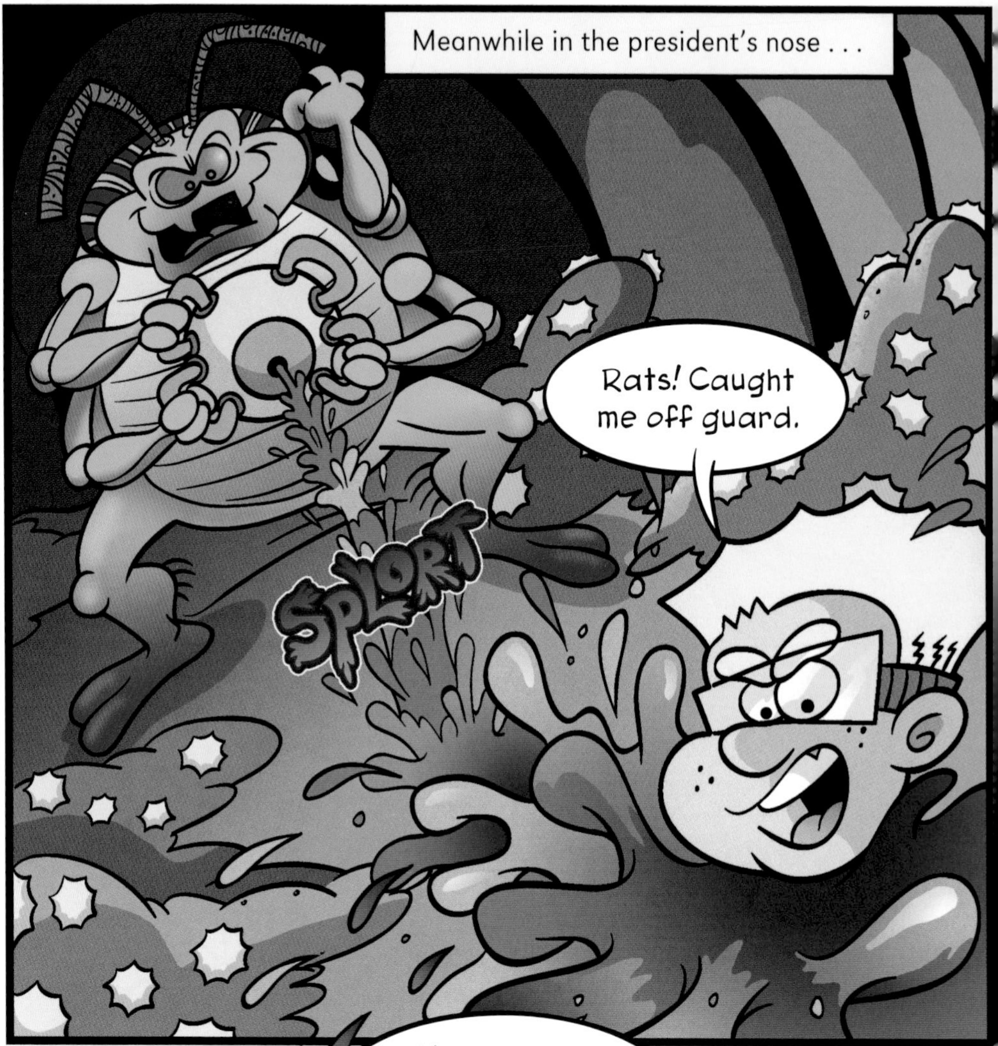
Meanwhile in the president's nose . . .
Rats! Caught me off guard.
SPLORT

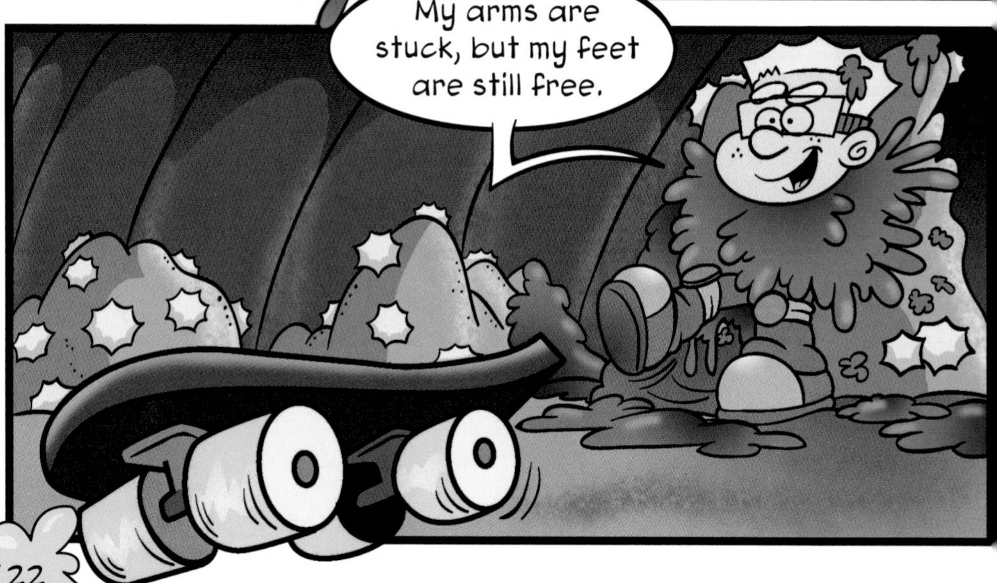
My arms are stuck, but my feet are still free.

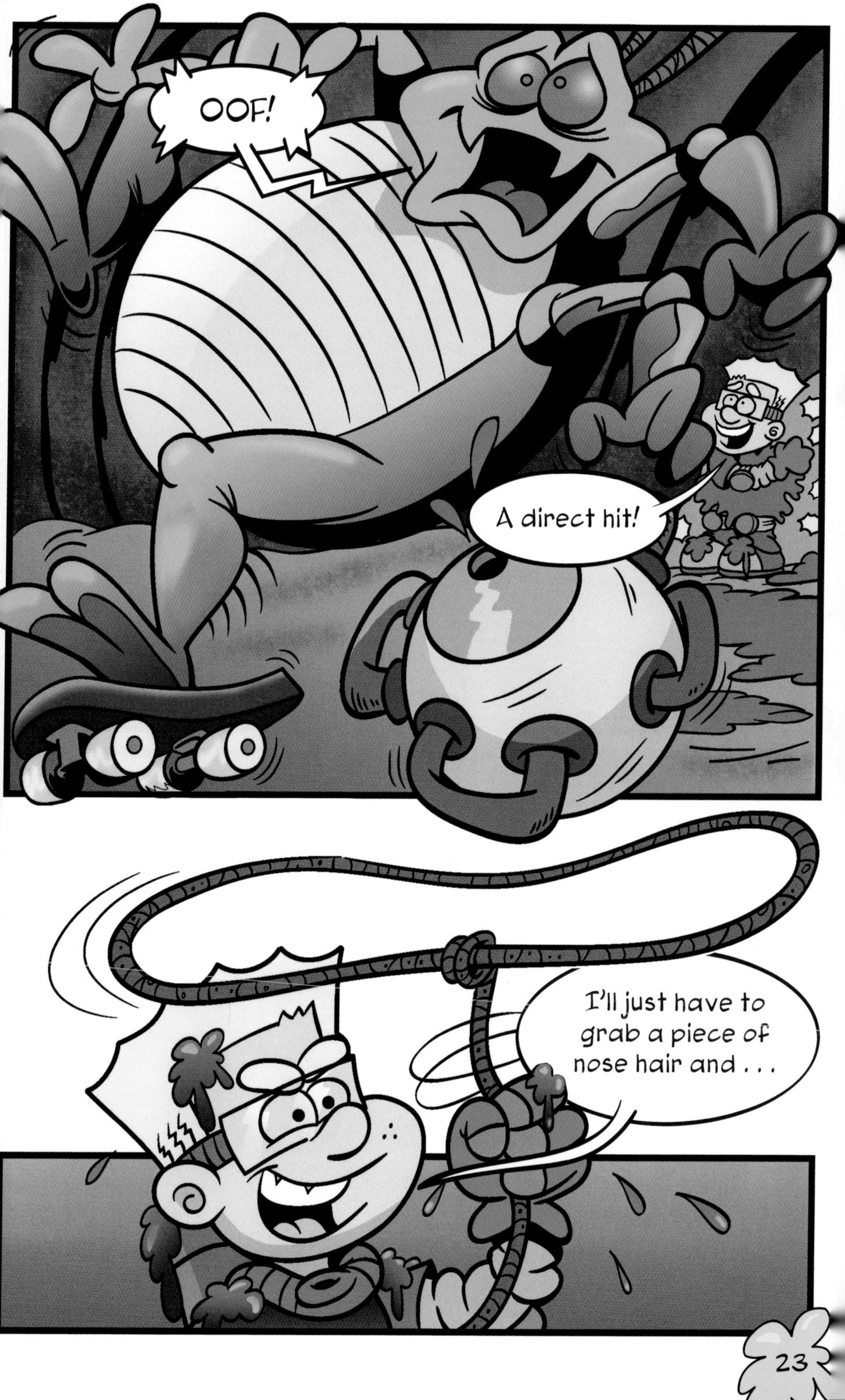
OOF!
A direct hit!
I'll just have to grab a piece of nose hair and . . .

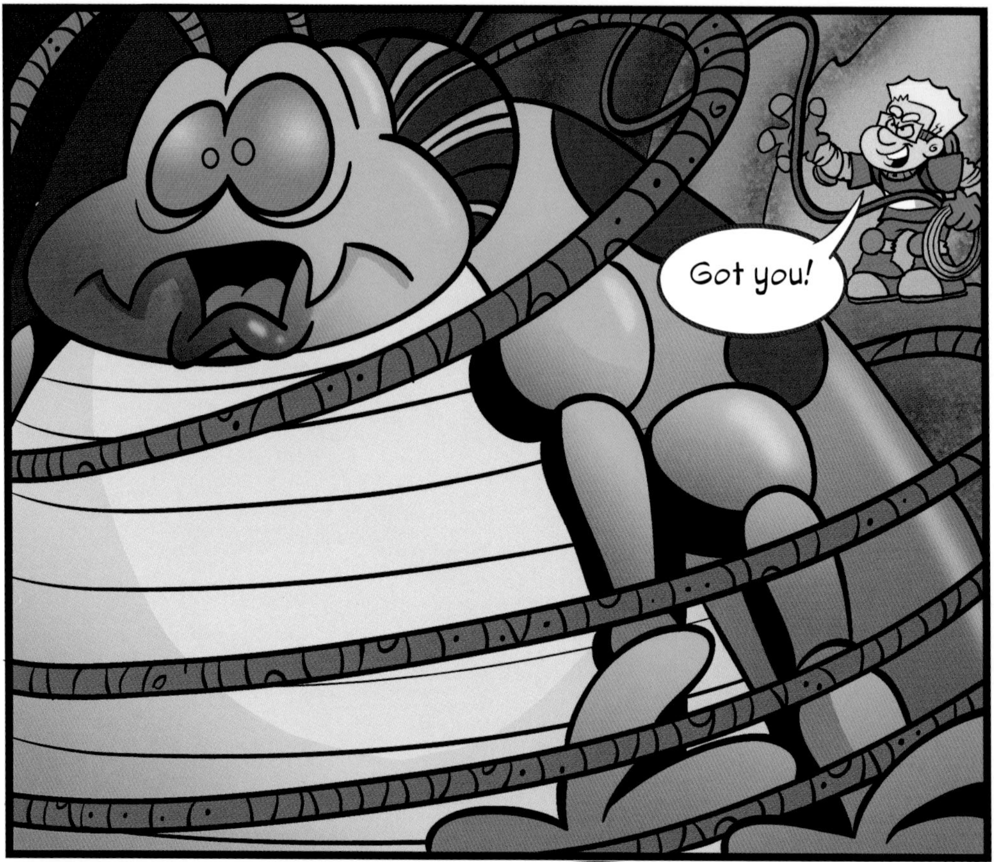
Got you!

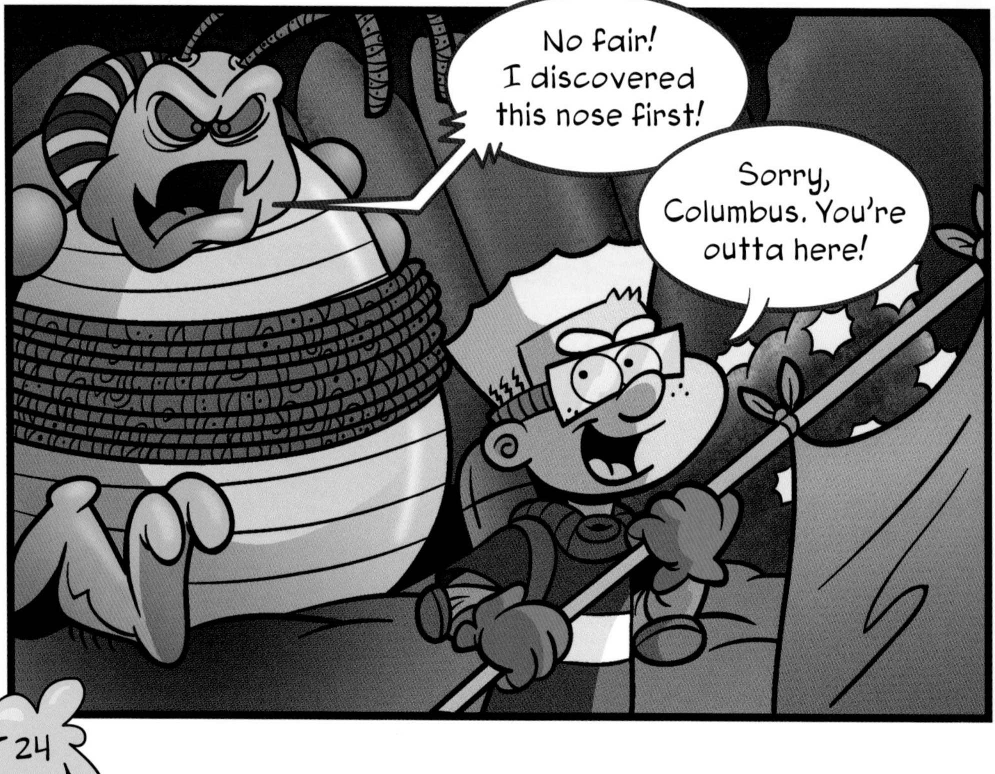
No fair! I discovered this nose first!
Sorry, Columbus. You're outta here!

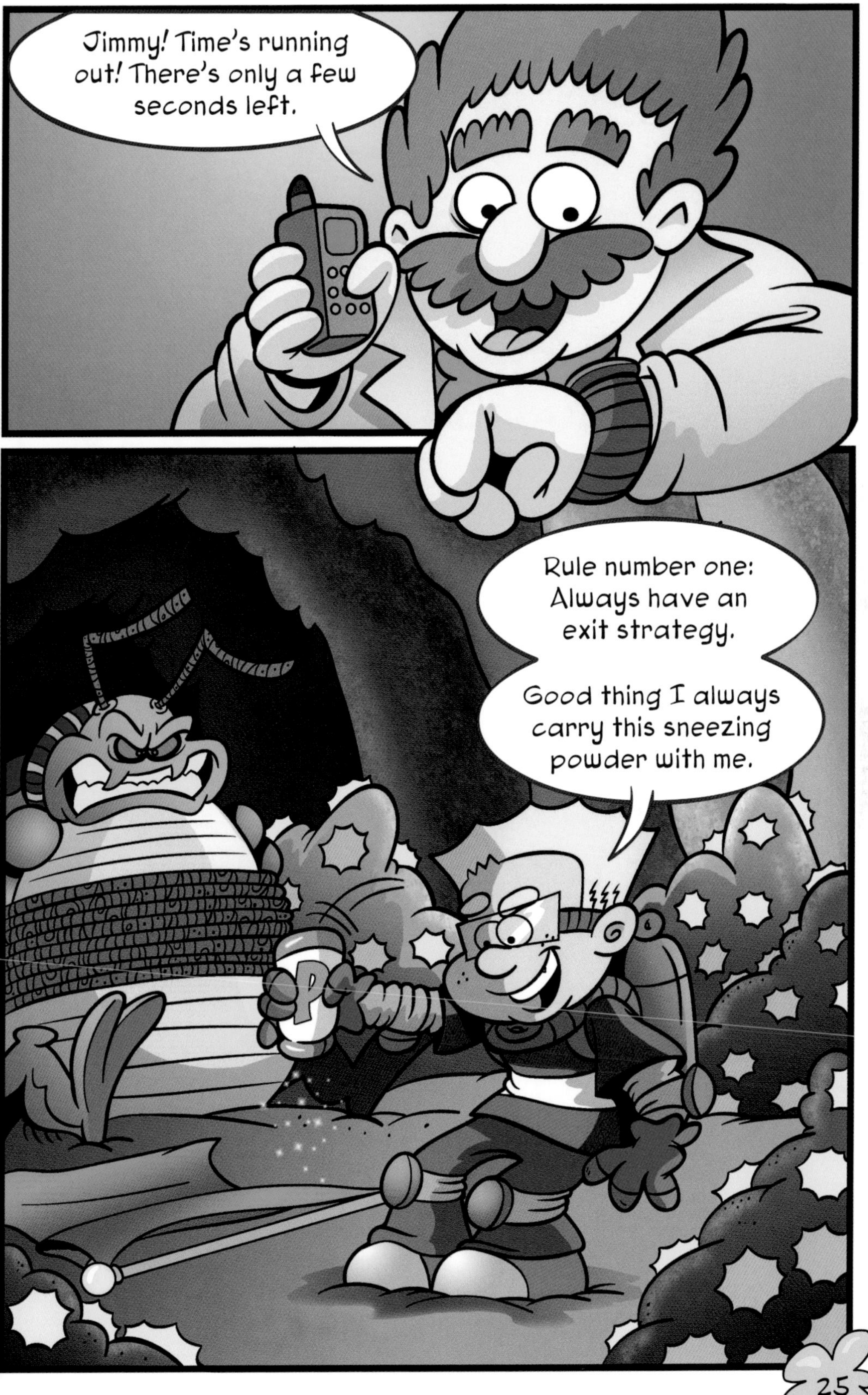
Jimmy! Time's running out! There's only a few seconds left.
Rule number one: Always have an exit strategy.
Good thing I always carry this sneezing powder with me.

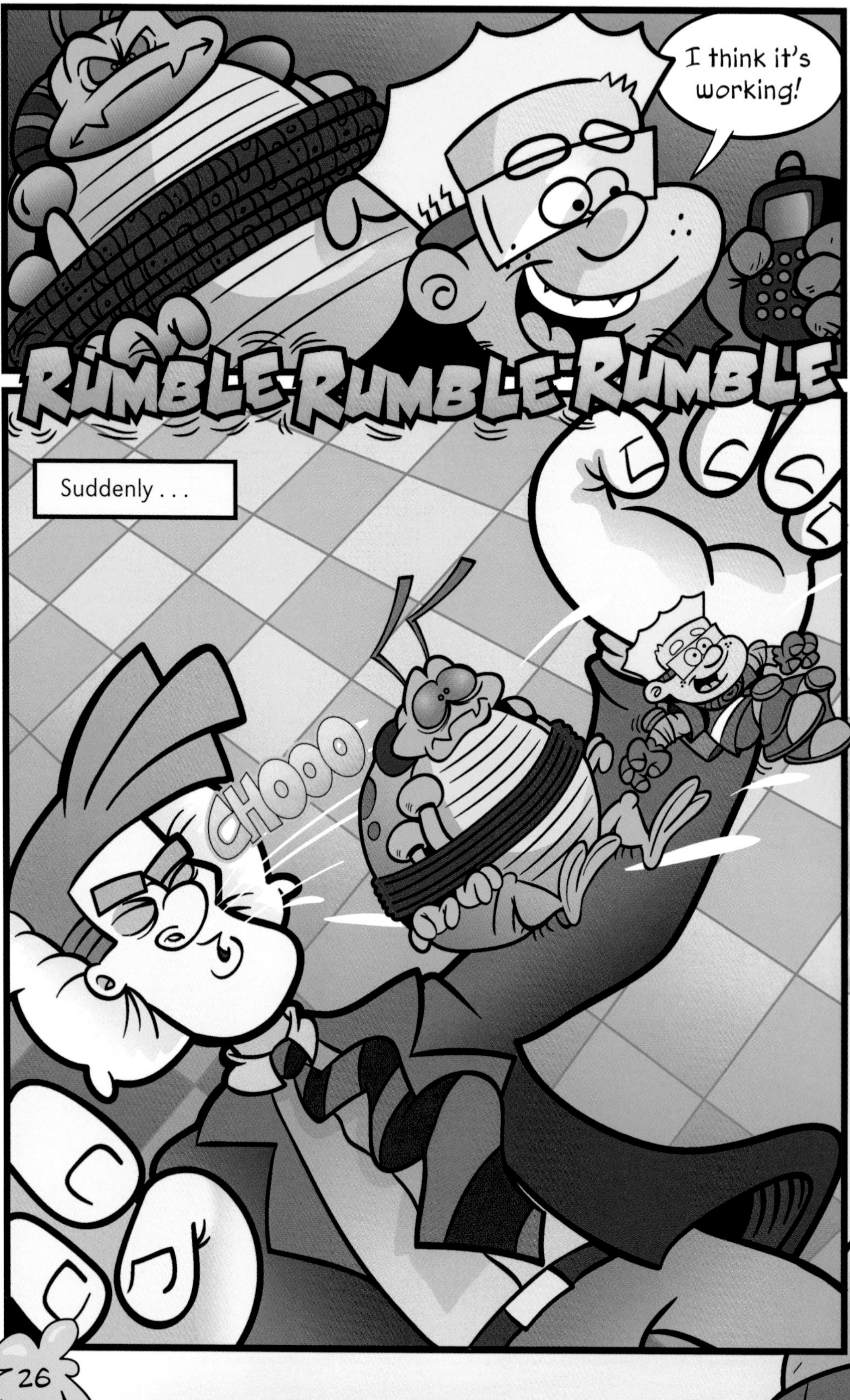
I think it's working!
RUMBLE RUMBLE RUMBLE
Suddenly . . .
CHOOO

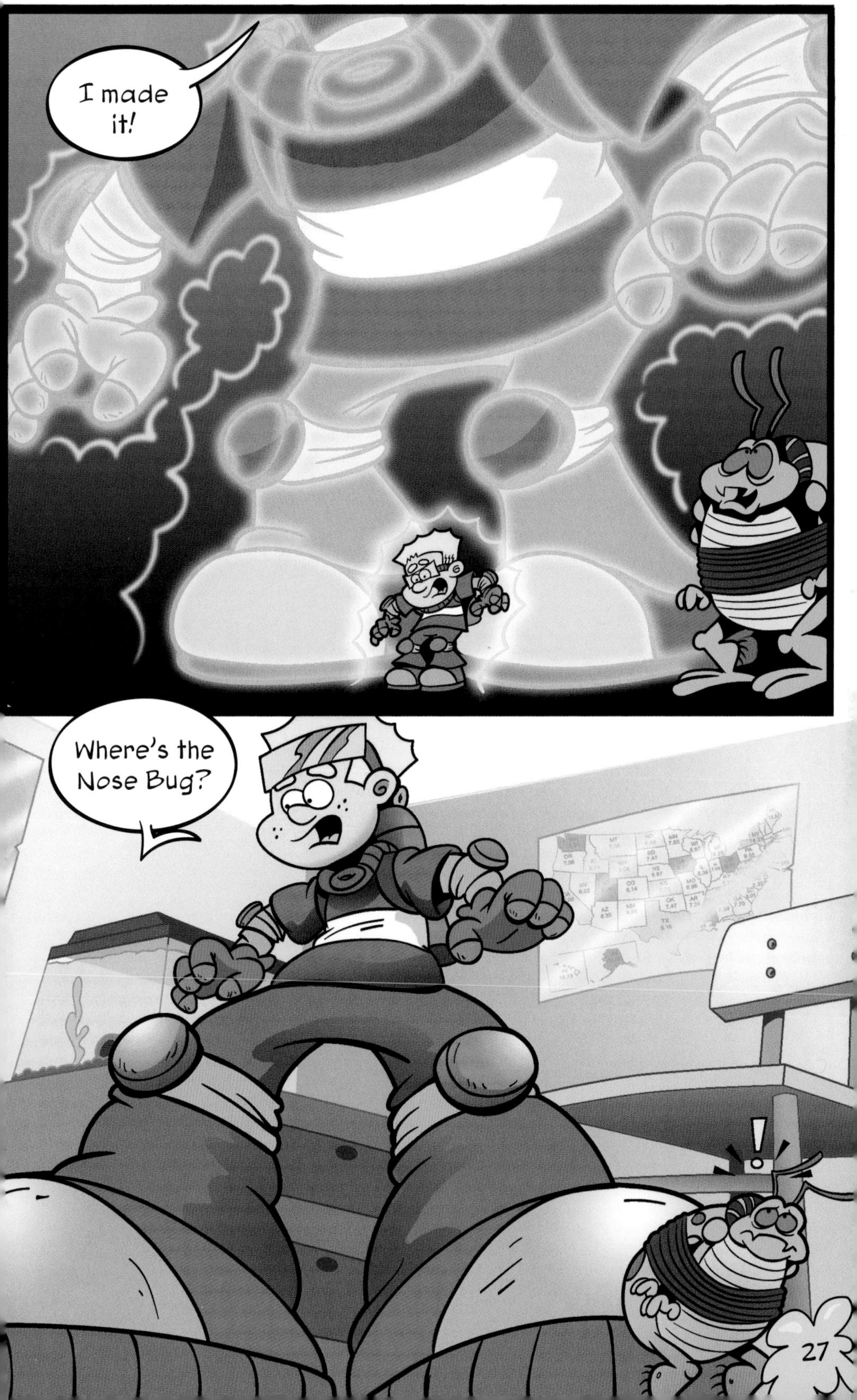
I made it!
Where's the Nose Bug?
!

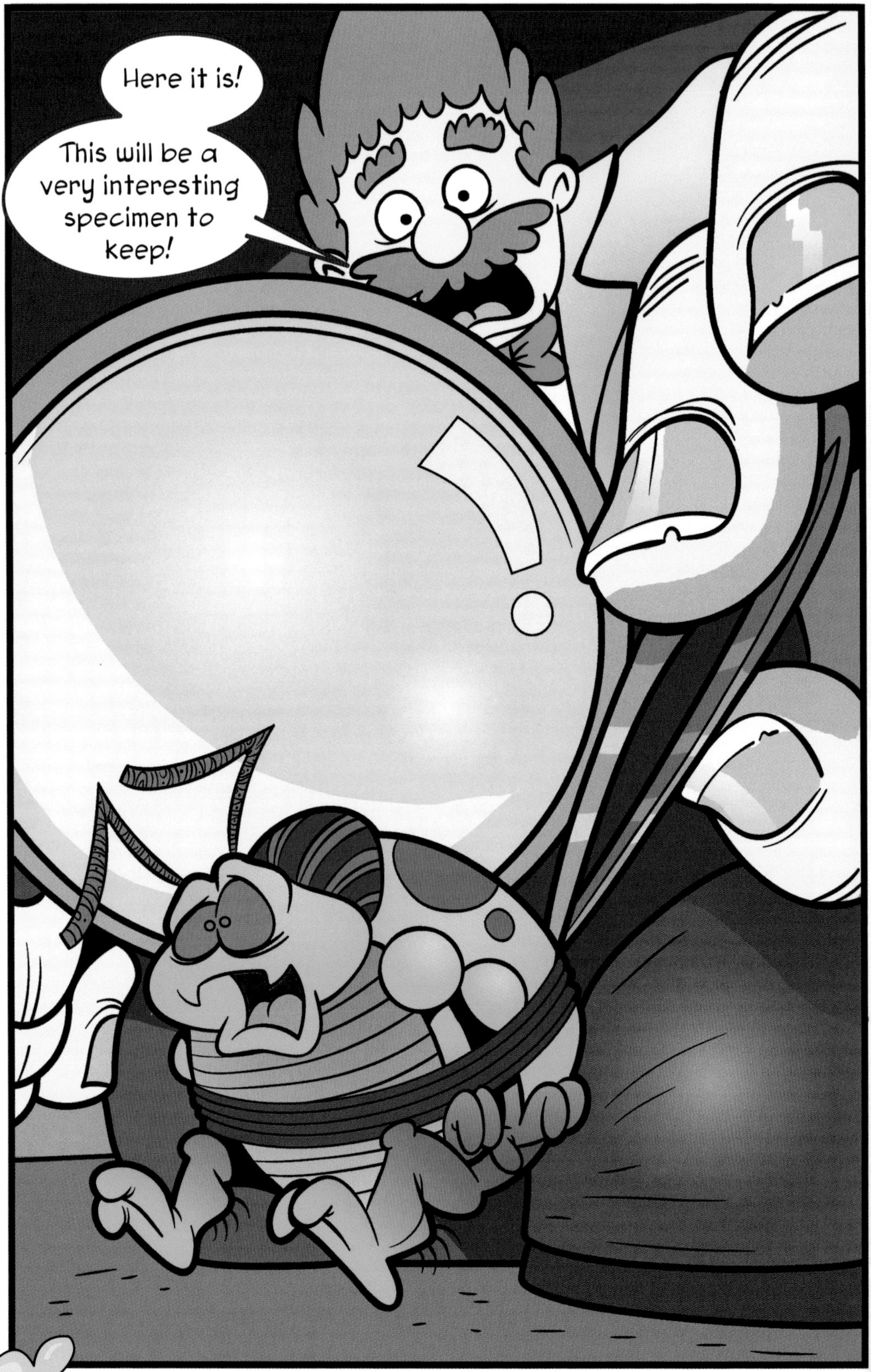
Here it is!
This will be a very interesting specimen to keep!

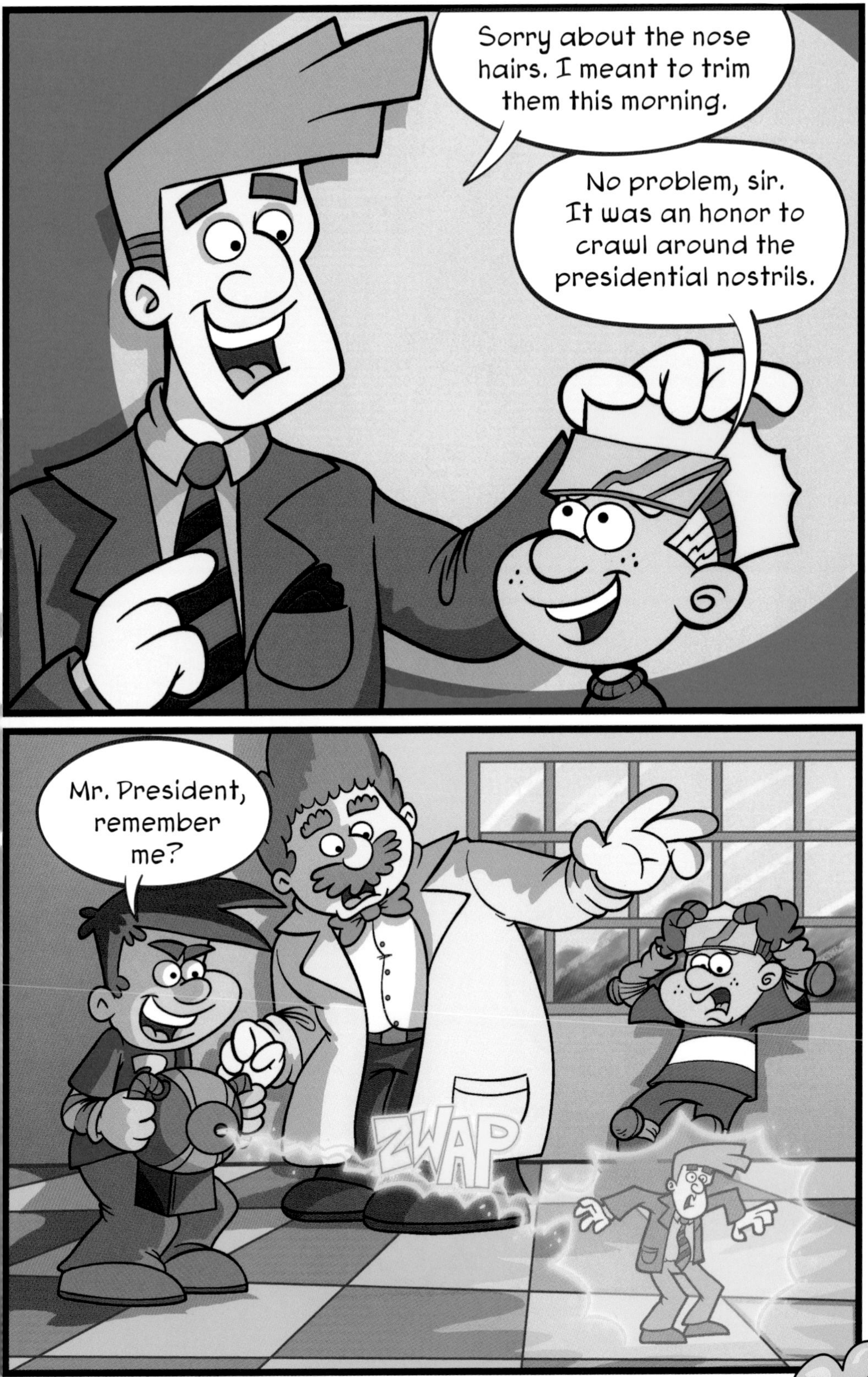
Sorry about the nose hairs. I meant to trim them this morning.
No problem, sir. It was an honor to crawl around the presidential nostrils.
Mr. President, remember me?
ZWAP

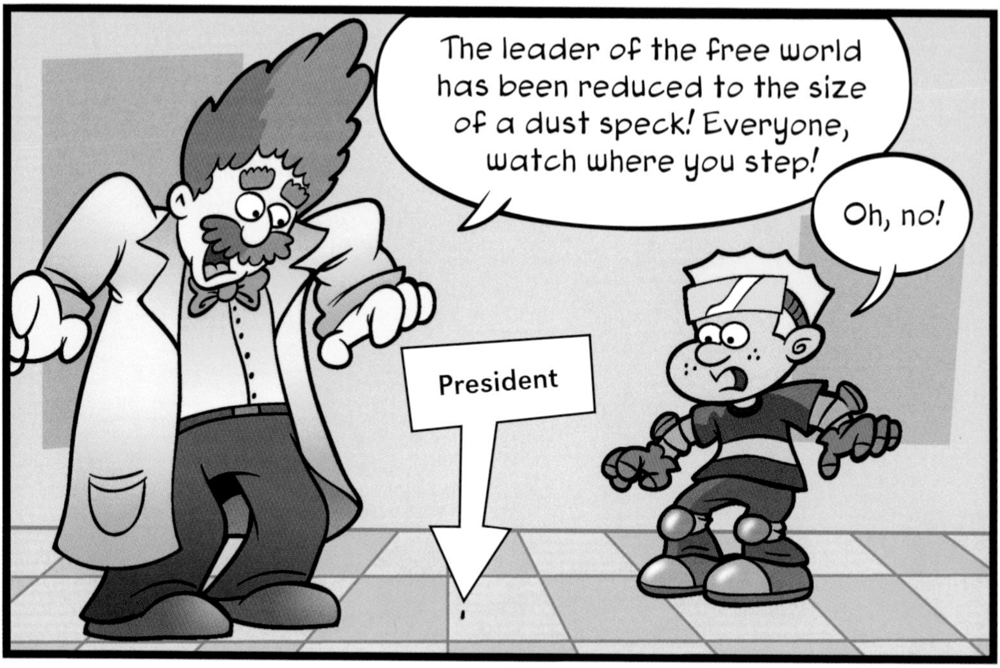
The leader of the free world has been reduced to the size of a dust speck! Everyone, watch where you step!
Oh, no!
President

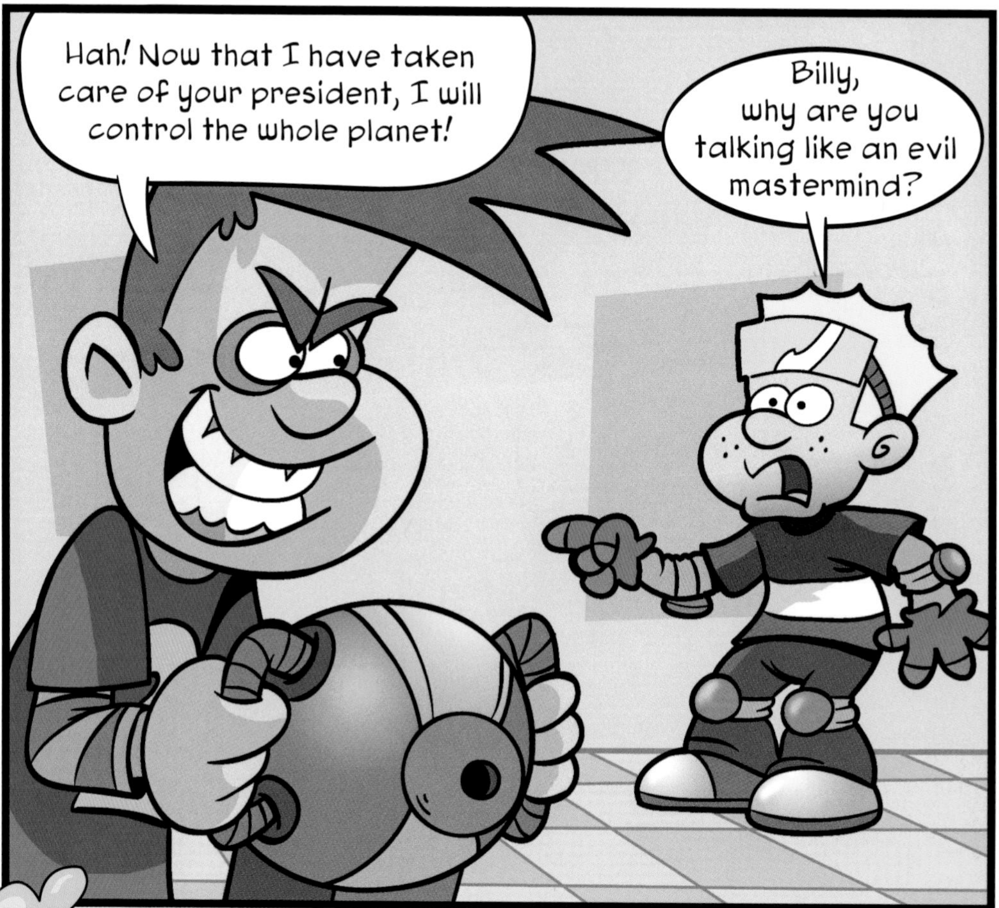
Hah! Now that I have taken care of your president, I will control the whole planet!
Billy, why are you talking like an evil mastermind?

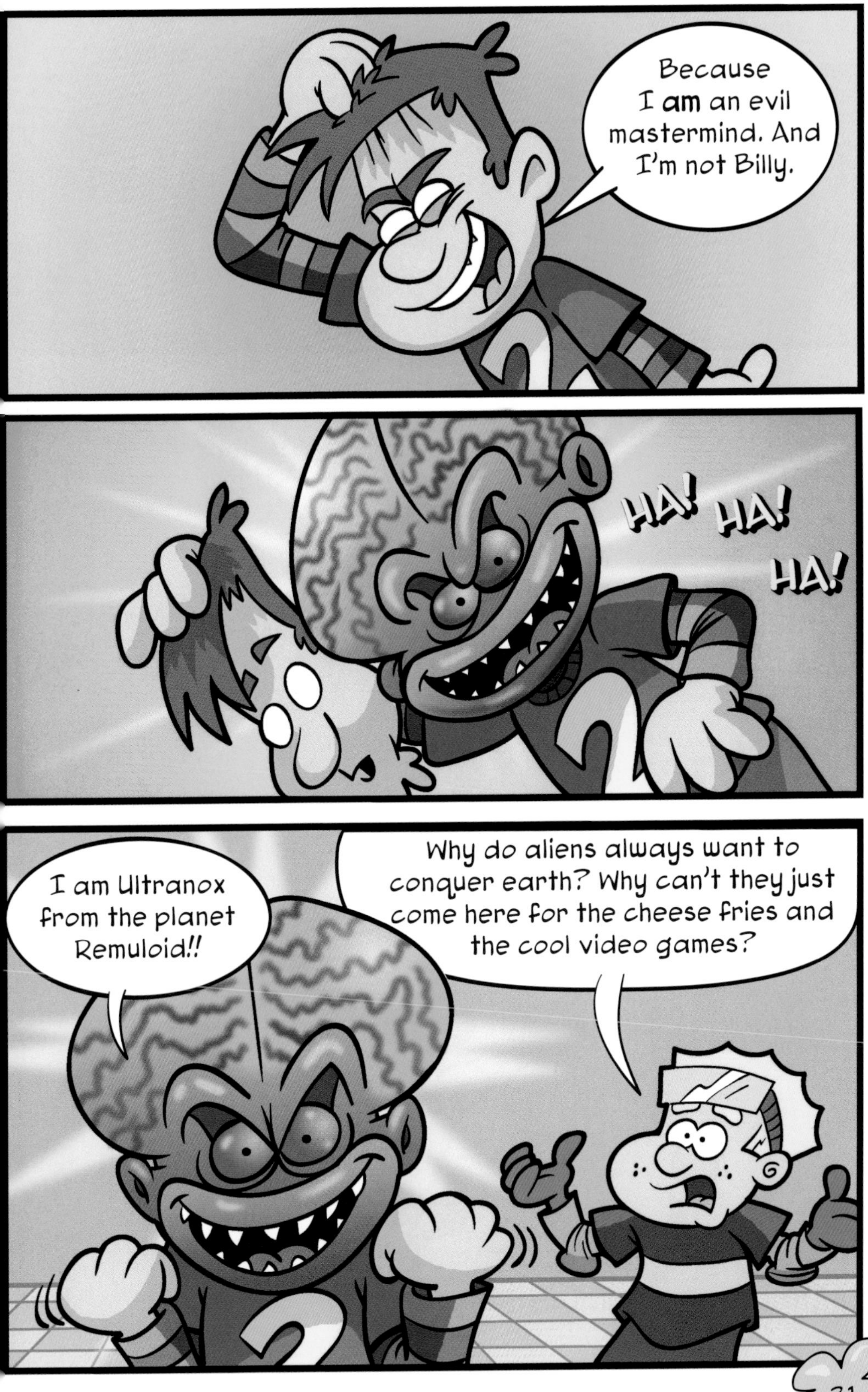
Because I **am** an evil mastermind. And I'm not Billy.
HA! HA! HA!
I am Ultranox from the planet Remuloid!!
Why do aliens always want to conquer earth? Why can't they just come here for the cheese fries and the cool video games?

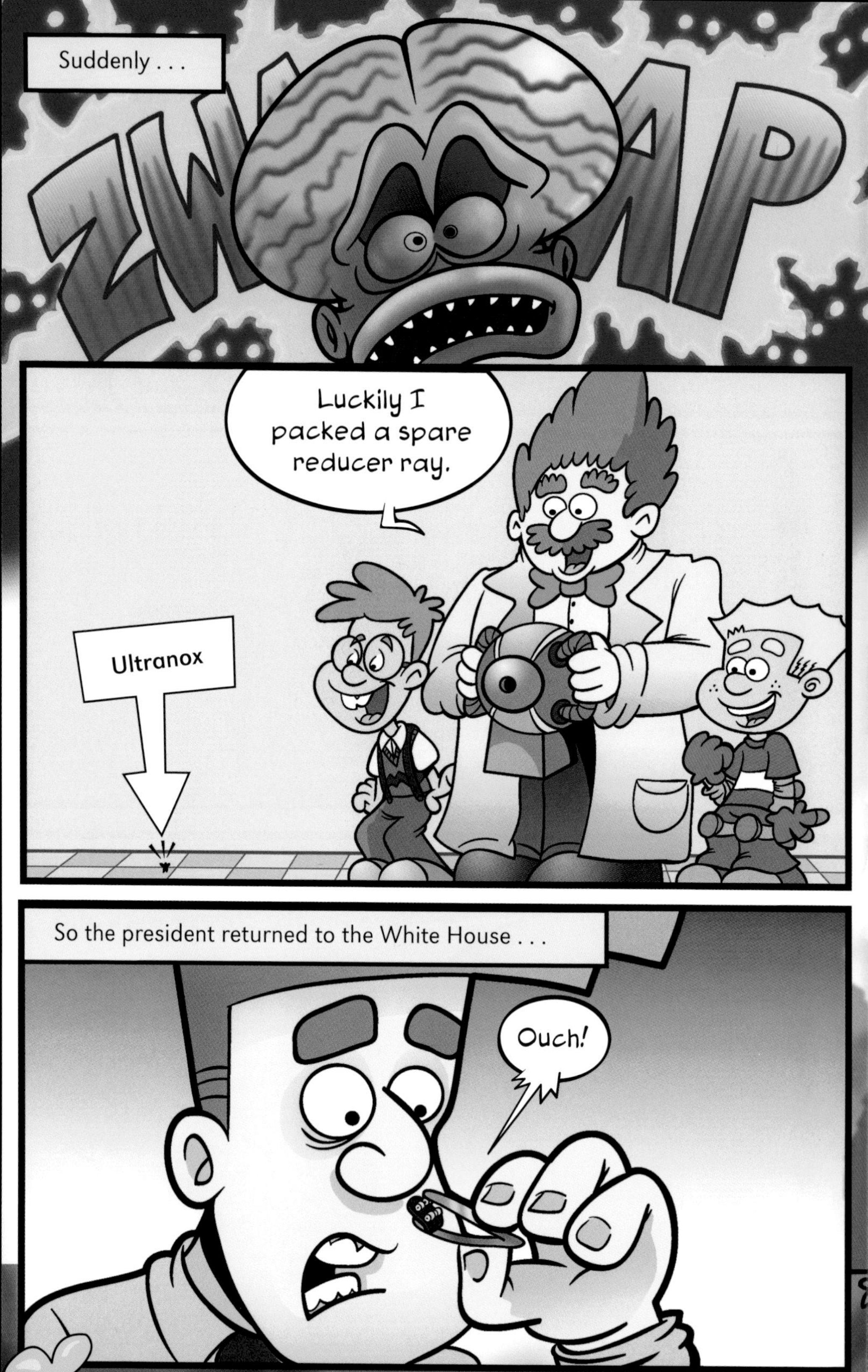

Suddenly . . .
ZWAP
Luckily I packed a spare reducer ray.
Ultranox
So the president returned to the White House . . .
Ouch!

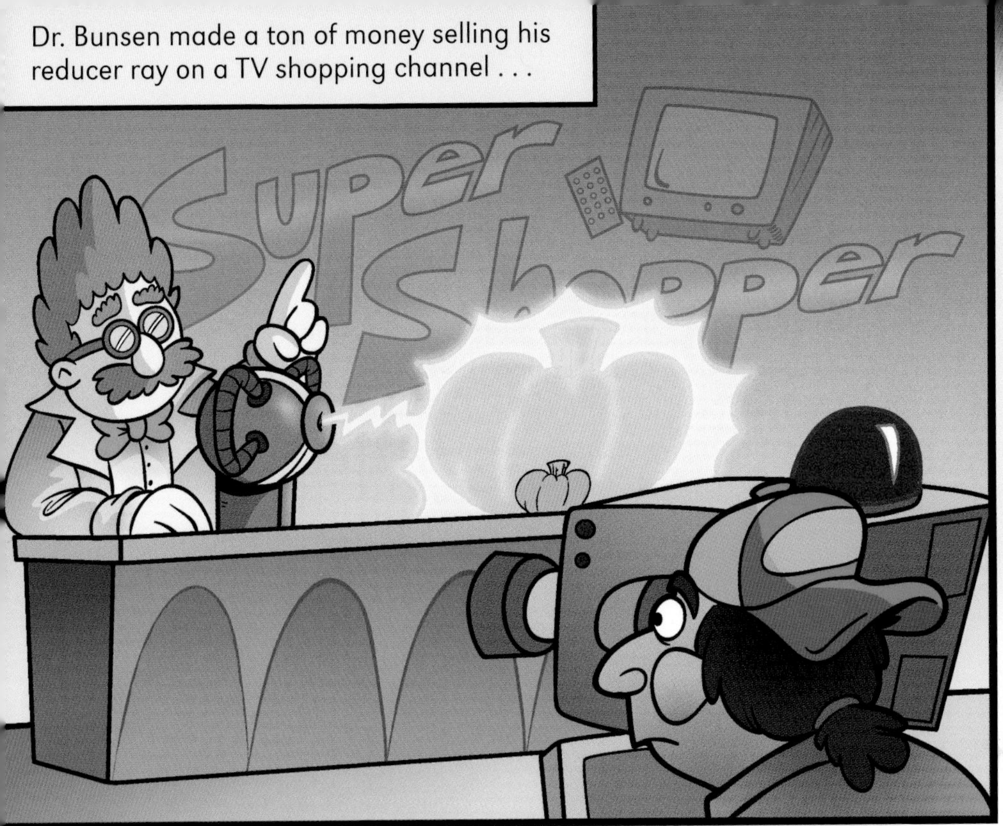
Dr. Bunsen made a ton of money selling his reducer ray on a TV shopping channel . . .
Super Shopper

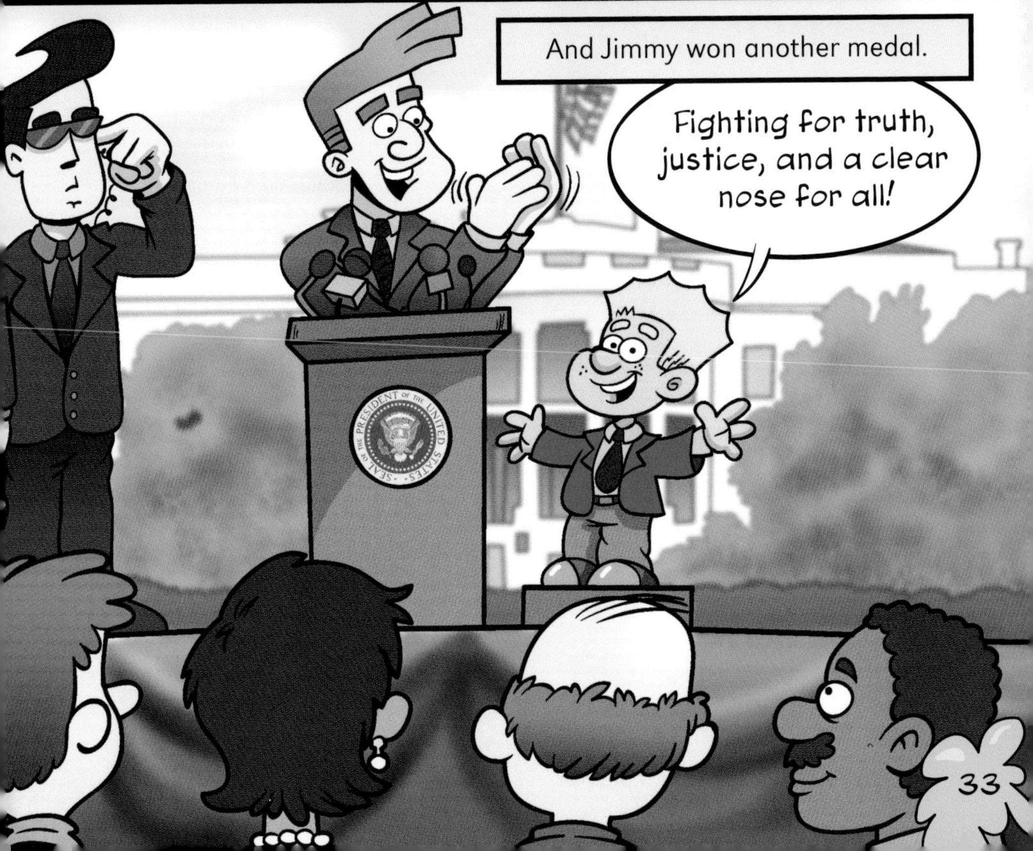
And Jimmy won another medal.
Fighting for truth, justice, and a clear nose for all!
SEAL OF THE PRESIDENT OF THE UNITED STATES

ABOUT THE AUTHOR

Born in 1962 in Denver, Colorado, Scott Nickel works by day at Paws, Inc., Jim Davis's famous Garfield studio, and he freelances by night. Burning the midnight oil, Scott has created hundreds of humorous greeting cards and written several children's books, short fiction for *Boys' Life* magazine, comic strips, and lots of really funny knock-knock jokes. He was raised in southern California, but in 1995 Scott moved to Indiana, where he currently lives with his wife, two sons, six cats, and several sea monkeys.

ABOUT THE ILLUSTRATOR

Steve Harpster has loved drawing funny cartoons, mean monsters, and goofy gadgets since he was able to pick up a pencil. In first grade, instead of writing a report about a dogsled story set in Alaska, Steve made a comic book about it. He was worried the teacher might not like it, but she hung it up for all the kids in the class to see. "It taught me to take a chance and try something different," says Steve. Steve landed a job drawing funny pictures for books. Now, he lives in Columbus, Ohio, with his wonderful wife, Karen, and their sheepdog, Doodle.

GLOSSARY

allergic reaction (uh-LUR-jik ree-AK-shuhn)—a nasty response to something you eat or breathe; allergic reactions can include sneezing, coughing, or even a bumpy rash.

conquer (KONG-kur)—to take control of an area or to defeat an enemy, like an alien in somebody's nose

infomercial (in-foh-MUR-shuhl)—a really, really, long TV commercial that tries to sell a product

microscopic (mye-kruh-SKOP-ik)—too small to see without a microscope

mucus (MYOO-kuhss)—a slippery slime that protects the inside of the nose, throat, and mouth

national security (NASH-uh-nuhl suh-KYOO-ruh-tee)—the safety and wellness of a country. Nasal (NAY-zul) security would be the safety of your nose.

nostrils (NOSS-truhlz)—the two openings in your nose that you breathe through; also, a great place for Flemzots to hide.

KNOW ABOUT YOUR NOSE

Did you know, the nose is more than just a bump with two holes? Many different parts help make your schnozz a super sniffer. Here are just a few:

Nostrils (NOSS-truhl)

Yep, those two holes actually have a name. The nostrils allow air to pass in and out of the nose. Inside each nostril, hair and mucus (also called snot) catch dirt and harmful germs.

Septum (SEP-tuhm)

This flexible piece of bone and tissue separates the two nostrils.

Nasal Cavity (NAY-zuhl KAV-uh-tee)

Once air travels through the nostrils, it reaches this large open space. The nasal cavity cleans the air again but also warms it up. Breathing in really cold air could damage your lungs. You could say the nasal cavity prevents lung freeze!

Olfactory Bulb (ahl-FAK-tuh-ree BUHLB)

This part is located above the nasal cavity and just below the brain. The olfactory bulb sends signals to the brain where they're identified as smells. Without this part, we wouldn't know the scent of an orange from the stink of a wet dog.

Allergies

Sometimes, things in the air can make parts of the nose go haywire. Allergies can cause people to snort, sniffle, and sneeze. Some of the most common allergies include pollen, mold, pets, and . . . dust mites!

Dust mites are microscopic bugs, sort of like those pesky Flemzots. You can't see them, but 100,000 to 10 million of them are usually crawling on your mattress. Yuck!

Luckily, vacuuming your room and washing your sheets can help get rid of the little critters. So, keep it clean, and you'll be less likely to sneeze.

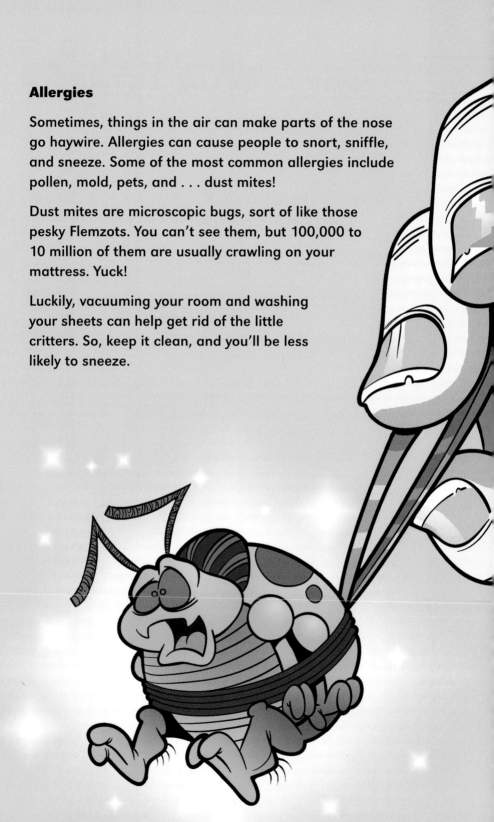

DISCUSSION QUESTIONS

1.) Jimmy takes a risk to help the president. Are risks good or bad? Can you think of an example of both a good risk and a bad risk?

2.) Jimmy is almost trapped in the president's nose. Luckily, he always carries some sneezing powder. What things do you carry or wear every day? How do they help you?

3.) At the end, Jimmy wins a medal. He says, "Fighting for truth, justice, and a clear nose for all!" Think of something completely different for him to say here. How would you end the story?

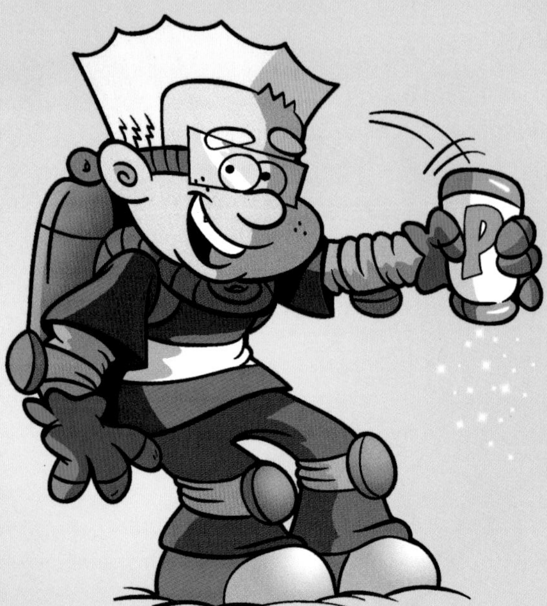
P

WRITING PROMPTS

1.) Skateboarding inside the president's nose is pretty gross. Make a list of the three grossest things you've ever done. Pick one, and write about that moment.

2.) At the end of the story, Dr. Bunsen makes a ton of money by selling his reducer ray. If you could buy one, what would you do with it? Describe some of the adventures you would have.

3.) Ultranox and Flemzot are both from the planet Remuloid. What do you think that planet is like? Write a story about Remuloid and the creatures that live there.

INTERNET SITES

Do you want to know more about subjects related to this book? Or are you interested in learning about other topics? Then check out FactHound, a fun, easy way to find Internet sites.

Our investigative staff has already sniffed out great sites for you!

Here's how to use FactHound:

1. Visit *www.facthound.com*

2. Select your grade level.

3. To learn more about subjects related to this book, type in the book's ISBN number: **159889837X**.

4. Click the **Fetch It** button.

FactHound will fetch the best Internet sites for you!